Pr...
the Blu...

"The Bluford Serie...
— Adam A.

"These books are *deep*. They show readers who are going through difficult problems that they are not alone in the world. And they even help teach you how to deal with situations in a positive way."
— Vianny C.

"I want to confess something: before I started reading the Bluford Series, I didn't like to read at all. Now I can't stop."
— Mariela M.

"Each Bluford book starts out with a bang. And then, when you turn the page, it gets even better!"
— Alex M.

"These books are intense! When I read them, I feel like I am in the story and everything is happening to me."
— Cyntera L.

"These arc life-changing stories that make you think long after you reach the last page."
— Eddie M.

"I found it very easy to lose myself in these books. They kept my interest from beginning to end and were always realistic. The characters are vivid, and the endings left me in eager anticipation of the next book."
— Keziah J.

"For the first time in high school, I read a book I liked. For real, the Bluford Series is *tight*."

—*Jermaine B.*

"These are thrilling, suspenseful books filled with real-life scenarios that make them too good to put down."

—*DeAndria B.*

"My school is just like Bluford High. The characters are just like people I know. These books are *real!*"

—*Jessica K.*

"I thought the Bluford Series was going to be boring, but once I started, I couldn't stop reading. I had to keep going just to see what would happen next. Now I'm done, and I can't wait for more books."

—*Jamal C.*

"Each Bluford book gives you a story that could happen to anyone. The details make you feel like you are inside the books. The storylines are amazing and realistic. I loved them all."

—*Elpiclio B.*

"One of my friends told me how good the Bluford Series is. She was right. Once I started reading, I couldn't stop, not even to sleep!"

—*Bibi R.*

"I love the Bluford books and the stories they tell. They're so real and action-packed, I feel like I'm inside the pages, standing next to the characters!"

—*Michael D.*

Pretty Ugly

Karyn Langhorne Folan

Series Editor: Paul Langan

TOWNSEND PRESS

www.townsendpress.com

Books in the Bluford Series

Copyright © 2011 by Townsend Press, Inc.
Printed in the United States of America

9 8 7 6 5 4 3

Cover illustration © 2011 by Gerald Purnell

Townsend Press, Inc.
439 Kelley Drive
West Berlin, NJ 08091
permissions@townsendpress.com

ISBN-13: 978-1-59194-233-7
ISBN-10: 1-59194-233-0

Library of Congress Control Number:
2010934777

Chapter 1

F
The letter was scrawled so big and red, Jamee wondered if Mrs. Guessner had any ink left in her pen after she had made it.

The grade covered up the first three questions on the algebra test. The words "See me" covered up two more wrong answers. At the bottom, a long red line was scratched on the paper with the words "Parent's signature" printed beneath it.

Jamee crumpled the test into her fist. Mrs. Guessner was at the front of the room going over the answers, but Jamee was too mad to listen.

Stupid, stupid, stupid, she wanted to scream. *Why is school so stupid?*

"Jamee?"

Jamee didn't answer, hoping that the

teacher would move on.

"Jamee?"

She rolled her eyes, shifted in her chair and gave Mrs. Guessner her best leave-me-alone face, but it didn't work.

"Can you tell us how to solve number eleven?"

Jamee sighed. *I failed, remember? What are you asking* me *for?* she wanted to say. Instead, she shook her head.

"No," she said simply.

"Come on," Mrs. Guessner urged. She sounded as if she was offering a treat. "You were one of the only people in this class to get this one right. Tell us how you did it."

Jamee glanced at the crumpled paper. Mrs. Guessner was right: number eleven was one of the few problems that didn't have a red "x" next to it, but Jamee wasn't sure why. She couldn't explain how she had gotten the right answer even if Mrs. Guessner offered to pay her.

Mrs. Guessner stared impatiently from her desk at the front of the room. The class suddenly grew quiet. Jamee felt as if an imaginary spotlight was shining on her.

"I got it right because . . ." Jamee sat

up straight and imitated a smart girl, making sure to say each word carefully. "You forgot to erase it from the board before you handed out the test."

Several kids chuckled in disbelief. Jamee gave her head a little toss at the sound and nodded, smiling.

Mrs. Guessner frowned.

"You really should take your schoolwork more seriously, Jamee," she said, shaking her head as if she was disappointed. "This is important—"

"Come on, Mrs. Guessner," Jamee snapped. "Ain't nobody gonna ask me to solve for x in real life. They might ask me a lot of things, but 'solve for x' ain't gonna be one of them!"

There was more laughter. Jamee even heard someone snort.

"Well," Mrs. Guessner's voice rose. "That's where you're wrong. We use algebra a lot in the real world. For example—"

The bell rang, and her words were drowned out by chairs scraping the floor.

"I'm offering a retake of this test on Thursday after school!" the teacher called over the noise. "And there will be help sessions after school every day starting today!"

Half the class was already out the door. Jamee tried to sneak out too, but Mrs. Guessner called out, "Wait, Jamee. Just a minute. I want to talk to you."

Jamee sighed. "My next class is gym, Mrs. Guessner," she began. "I gotta get all the way to the other end of the school and get changed and—"

"I'll give you a pass," Mrs. Guessner replied, filling out a hall pass as she spoke. "You need to make sure you retake the test on Thursday. And I want you to come for help this afternoon."

"But I can't!" Jamee cried. "Cheerleading tryouts start today!"

"You won't be a cheerleader if you don't pass this class," Mrs. Guessner warned, her voice stern. "It's disturbing to see a student performing this badly so early in the year." She shook her head as if she was surprised at what she was saying. "Especially *you*. When I saw your name on my class roster, I thought you'd be more like your sister, Darcy . . ."

Darcy.

Jamee felt as if something hot and prickly had been dumped over her head. Mrs. Guessner was still talking, but once she said the *D* word, Jamee couldn't hear her anymore.

4

Darcy.

For the first few days at Bluford High School, Jamee thought it was almost cool to have a sister in the junior class and older kids asking, "Are you Darcy Wills's sister?" But that feeling lasted about a week. Then the whole "Darcy's sister" thing started to become just like Darcy: a pain in Jamee's backside.

It started in history with Mr. Gonzalez. "You need to study harder, like your sister Darcy," he had said as he placed a graded test on her desk. A large angry *D* was circled in blue ink.

And in English a couple of days later, the same thing happened: "You're not as good a writer as your sister Darcy."

And then again in physical science: "If you're having trouble, maybe you could ask your sister Darcy."

If the teachers weren't bad enough, at least once a day juniors or seniors Jamee didn't know would stop her and ask, "Hey, aren't you Darcy Wills's sister?" Then they would add a comment like "You look just like her" or "You don't look anything like her." Each time, they would grin as if what they said was a compliment.

Darcy, Darcy, Darcy.

"Did you know Darcy was in my honors algebra class her freshman year?" Mrs. Guessner smiled as if she was reliving a pleasant memory. "She's one of the best students I ever had at Bluford."

"Well, I'm not Darcy." The words stung as Jamee said them. She didn't mean to sound rude, but she couldn't help it. Mrs. Guessner blinked.

"I know that, Jamee," she said gently. "All I'm saying is, you can do better. Right now it's as if you're not even trying. You realize cheerleaders have to maintain their grades, right? If your average falls below a C, you won't be able to join the squad, no matter what," Mrs. Guessner explained.

"I know," Jamee mumbled, crossing her arms and trying her best not to say anything that would get her in more trouble.

"Now, I know you struggled last year in middle school," Mrs. Guessner continued. "I understand your guidance counselor and your parents met just before school started—"

"Yeah, I know. I was there," Jamee interrupted, wishing she could just forget the meeting in August when she crowded in Mr. Dorber's stuffy office

6

with her parents.

"I noticed Jamee had some academic problems in middle school. If she's going to make it through Bluford, we're really going to have to stay on top of things," Mr. Dorber had said, flipping through a folder with her name on it.

Jamee had felt as if she was trapped in a cage. She wondered how many details of her life were in Mr. Dorber's folder.

Did he know Dad had walked out on the family five years ago and just came back last year? Did he know while Dad was gone, she had hung out with the troubled kids, people who didn't care one bit about grades or school? Did he know that last year she had even tried to run away? How could he know any of that?

"I'm going to suggest a lot of communication between home and school," Mr. Dorber had said, eyeing her as he spoke.

"Don't you worry. We're gonna stay on her about her schoolwork," Mom had agreed, nodding her head forcefully.

"Tell her teachers to call us anytime," Dad had added. "Especially if she starts falling behind."

Mr. Dorber had smiled and written

something in her file. *"That's good to hear, Mr. and Mrs. Wills. The transition to high school can be difficult. But if we all work together, Jamee will do as well at Bluford as her sister . . ."*

Just remembering the conversation made Jamee want to gag.

"I really want you to retake the test," Mrs. Guessner continued, breaking Jamee's thoughts. "And if I were you, I'd come for help today and tomorrow after school. You could even ask Darcy to look over your homework, too. She'll be able to help."

No, I'm not gonna do that! Jamee thought angrily. *I don't want her help. I'm NOT Darcy, okay, so get over it!* she wanted to scream. But even more, she wanted to get away from Mrs. Guessner.

"All right," Jamee said, doing her best to hide her frustration. "I'll try to stop by after school. And I'll definitely take the retest. But right now, I gotta go or I'll be late for gym."

Students were gathering outside the door waiting for Mrs. Guessner's next class. Jamee could see that the teacher noticed them. *Please just let me go*, she wanted to say.

"Okay, Jamee," Mrs. Guessner sighed,

handing her the hall pass. "I'll look for you after school. And don't forget to have your parents sign your test and bring it with you to class tomorrow. I want them to know how you're doing."

Great, Jamee thought to herself. She could already hear her mother's nagging and see the look of disappointment on her father's face. Maybe Darcy would sigh and shake her head at her, too. Jamee had watched her do that for years. The thought made Jamee's face burn.

Don't worry about it, Jamee told herself. *Just think about tryouts.* She closed her eyes and imagined spending the afternoon with her friend Amberlynn doing something she was good at— cheerleading. It was something Darcy could never do. The idea almost made her smile. She opened her eyes, glanced at the crumpled test, and turned to her teacher.

"Whatever you say, Mrs. Guessner."

As soon as the final bell rang, Jamee headed straight for the gym. The locker room was already crowded with girls when she arrived, most of them chatting nervously as they changed out of their school clothes.

9

"As soon as you're dressed, sign in and get your numbers!" yelled an older dark-skinned girl in workout shorts and a gold Bluford T-shirt.

Jamee changed quickly, crammed her backpack with her crumpled test into her locker, and rushed into the gym. A long table stretched just inside the entrance. Two other girls in Bluford Cheerleading T-shirts sat at the table. Jamee figured they were upperclassmen who made the squad last year.

"Write your name here," one of them instructed, pointing to a clipboard that held a yellow sign-up sheet. Jamee carefully printed her name on the form.

"Jamee *Wills* . . ." the girl read. "Are you Darcy Wills's sister? She's in my English class," she continued before Jamee could reply. "That girl is smart."

"Yeah, that's Darcy," Jamee muttered and started walking away.

"Wait!" the cheerleader called. She wrote a number on a white sticker and handed it to Jamee. "You're number seventeen." She smiled. "There are lots of girls trying out. The number is how Coach Seville keeps track of who's who. I'm Crystal, by the way. Good luck."

"Thanks," Jamee grumbled, sticking

10

her number to her T-shirt. Crystal seemed nice, but now Jamee was sure the cheerleaders would expect her to be like Darcy. She couldn't stand it.

No, I'm not gonna let Darcy ruin this, Jamee told herself as she sat down on the crowded bleachers.

"Jamee! Over here!" called a voice. Jamee whipped around to see Amberlynn Bailey sitting a few rows behind her, waving eagerly. Amberlynn patted to an empty space beside her. "Come up here!" she urged.

Jamee scampered up the bleachers beneath a row of Bluford banners and sat down next to her friend. "Girl, I am glad to see you," she said, dropping an arm around Amberlynn's shoulders. "For a minute, I was afraid you'd changed your mind."

"Are you serious?" Amberlynn asked, her braids dancing on her shoulders as she talked. "There's no way I'd miss this. I've wanted to cheer for Bluford every since Roylin's first game on the JV football team!" Roylin was Amberlynn's older brother.

"I know," Jamee laughed for what felt like the first time all day. "It's all you ever talked about last year. I was about to tape your mouth shut a few times."

"Well it worked, didn't it? We're both here, right?"

"Just like always," Jamee replied with a grin. She had been friends with Amberlynn since fifth grade. They met in Ms. Scanlon's language arts class at Irving Middle School. Back then, Dad was gone, and Mom was forced to work long hours at the hospital to pay the bills. To help out, Jamee's grandmother moved into their apartment. It was years before a massive stroke left her weak and confused. Besides cooking meals and making sure the girls got to school on time, Grandma checked every homework assignment. Sometimes Jamee complained.

"Baby girl, I wish I could be in school like you right now," Grandma would say. *"But since I can't, I want you to show me what they teachin' you. And if you can't show me, I'm gonna call your school up and ask 'em why."*

Jamee wasn't ever sure if Grandma meant it, but that year her grades went up. She got B's in every subject. While she couldn't compete with Darcy, she did well enough that Mom was satisfied. And, thanks to Amberlynn, she discovered something in which Darcy couldn't compete: cheerleading.

Jamee had been doing it ever since and hoped to continue it this year, no matter what Mrs. Guessner or anyone else said. Cheerleading was the only thing that hadn't really changed this year. Home was a different story.

Dad's return and promise to make up lost time to the family.

Grandma's sad death in her sleep early in the summer.

The sudden announcement of Mom's pregnancy.

Most nights Jamee stared at the ceiling, thinking about it all, her mind racing, her heart pounding. While she tried her best each day, sometimes she just felt lost. Pregnancy had slowed Mom down, leaving her distracted and cranky. Dad was working two jobs so they could afford all the things the baby would need. Yes, the family was together again, but somehow Jamee saw less of her parents than ever. And when they were home, all Mom and Dad talked about was the new baby and Darcy's SATs.

Jamee sometimes felt as if she had become invisible. Cheerleading was an anchor that stopped that. It was hers, not Darcy's. It was stable, not changing. She looked forward to it like an old friend.

Snap!

Jamee felt a pop just beneath her nose.

"Hello, Earth to Jamee? Did you hear me?" Amberlynn asked, snapping her fingers again.

Jamee blinked. "Sorry. What did you say?"

Amberlynn rolled her bright brown eyes and grinned. "I said we both have to make this team, so we can hang out together." She jabbed Jamee with a playful elbow. "So no sleeping out there. We got a lot of competition."

Jamee shook off her thoughts and looked around. The bleachers had filled with girls, each wearing a numbered sticker on her chest. It seemed every girl who had ever done a cartwheel had decided to come to the gym. Except for Tasha Jenkins, who sat a couple of rows down with some older-looking girls. Jamee didn't see anyone from her middle school squad.

"Wow, there are enough girls here to make about five cheering squads," Jamee murmured, feeling suddenly nervous.

"It's true. You gotta figure that most of the girls who were on the squad last year will make it again," Amberlynn said softly. "That means only, like, six of us will make it."

Jamee took a deep breath. She had been a good cheerleader in middle school, but she knew Bluford was going to be a whole new world, just like her classes. For a split second, she remembered that she was supposed to meet Mrs. Guessner after school.

But then Coach Seville strode into the gym. There was no turning back now.

Chapter 2

"Welcome, ladies!"

Coach Seville, the advisor for the cheering squad, was a petite lady who had once been a gymnast. Jamee had heard rumors that she had gone to the Olympics when she was younger, but she was pretty sure that couldn't be right. People who had competed in the Olympics didn't end up at Bluford High, she figured.

"I'm glad to see so many of you interested in cheering on Bluford's Varsity squad," she shouted. Jamee was surprised at how loud her voice was: the tiny woman could bellow across the gym as if she had a microphone.

"But cheerleading isn't about wearing cute uniforms. It is a sport—the most dangerous one in high school.

Cheerleaders are *athletes*, as much as football players or basketball players. And as athletes, cheerleaders are expected to work as a team, to maintain a solid grade point average, and to reach for excellence. So if you're here for a cute uniform, let me tell you right now, this is *not* the place for you. You might as well leave right now."

She paused. The gym was quiet and tense. Jamee's legs twitched with nervous energy.

"We're going to spend the next couple of days teaching you routines and jumps. Then, on Thursday, you'll perform for me in small groups of three or four. Finally, on Friday, I'll post the list of girls who've made the Varsity squad on the bulletin board outside. Everyone know where that is?"

The crowd of girls mumbled and nodded from the bleachers.

"Now in a few minutes, our captains—Crystal, Michelle, and Julesa—will teach you a routine. You'll have some time to practice it today, to ask questions, to learn it. Tomorrow, we'll work on jumps. At the minimum, you must be able to do a toe-touch, a herkie, a pike, and splits. If you don't know

17

what those are," she smiled, "you'll find out tomorrow. If you know any tumbling—gymnastics—you'll definitely want to make sure you show me that by the time you and your group perform. Wednesday you'll have a chance to put everything together and get any extra help before Thursday's auditions. Does everyone understand?"

There were some quiet murmurs from the girls in the stands.

Coach Seville shook her head as if she was a little disappointed. "Ladies, you're going to have to do better than that," she said. "Crystal! Michelle! Julesa!" she bellowed. "Show 'em."

"Yes, Coach!" the girls boomed.

"Better." She turned toward the stands again. "Now let me hear you!"

"Yes, Coach!" Jamee and the other girls shouted. The gym rocked with the sounds of their voices.

"Okay. The co-captains will demonstrate, then it will be your turn."

Crystal and her two co-captains did a routine, first really fast, then slowly three more times. Jamee had never heard the chant, but she recognized a lot of the moves from middle school. They had worked a step dance routine into the middle of the cheer that wasn't familiar at all.

"That's the hard part," Amberlynn whispered. "That's how they're gonna weed us out."

Jamee nodded. It looked challenging.

"All right!" Coach Seville hollered. "Off your behinds and onto the floor!"

Jamee and the other girls lined up in long rows that covered the gym from one end to the other. Amberlynn stood on Jamee's left and a skinny girl in glasses took the place on her right. Crystal, Michelle, and Julesa stood in front of the large group.

"And ready?" Crystal cried.

"Ready!" Michelle and Julesa shouted back.

"Three, two, one . . . let's go!"

The routine was even more difficult than it looked from the bleachers. Jamee was soon struggling to keep the chant and the movements together in her mind. As tough as the cheer was, the step routine in the middle was even worse. The girl next to Jamee was having a really hard time. She jumped when she should have clapped, pivoted right when she should have moved left, and stomped when she should have slid to the side. At one point, she came too close to Jamee and stomped her foot so hard, Jamee felt her toes throbbing inside her shoes.

"Sorry," the girl mumbled each time she and Jamee bumped into each other. "Sorry." She sounded so nervous Jamee wondered how she had found the courage to try out.

"It's okay," Jamee said, but it really wasn't. There was no way this girl would make the Bluford cheerleading squad— even if she had a month to practice.

At last it was over.

"All right, ladies," Coach Seville boomed over them. "Does everyone have it?"

A few girls nodded, and a few others murmured quiet "yeahs." But the clumsy girl beside Jamee shouted out, "Yes, Coach!" She was so loud she sounded as if someone had stuck a pin in her.

Jamee heard snickering and turned her head. Tasha Jenkins had covered her mouth with her hand. She was standing beside one of the girls she had sat with on the bleachers, a tall girl with long, straight hair that didn't look real. She was really pretty but wore a lot of makeup. Jamee knew Mom would have said "Wash your face" if she had caught Jamee going out like that.

"Pathetic," the long haired girl murmured behind her hand.

"Who's that?" Jamee asked Amberlynn, careful to keep her voice down.

"Her name is Vanessa Pierce," Amberlynn whispered back. "She's a junior. She didn't make the squad last year. I heard she hasn't stopped practicing since then."

"How does Tasha know her?"

Amberlynn just shrugged.

There were a few more giggles, but then they suddenly stopped. Jamee looked up and saw that Coach Seville was approaching. She had a scowl on her face as she slowly paced closer and stopped in front of the nervous toe-stomping girl.

"That's what I want to hear! Enthusiasm!" Coach Seville said, squinting at the girl's yellow sticker. "Number thirty-five. What's your name?"

The girl pushed her glasses up her nose and grinned. "Angel," she replied. "Angel McAllister."

"Well, I like your spirit, Angel McAllister," Coach Seville said. "Spirit and enthusiasm are a big part of being a

21

good cheerleader."

"Thank you," Angel said.

"Suck up!" someone croaked from the back of the gym.

Angel hung her head. Jamee felt sorry for her, but in a way, the heckler was right. In spite of her loudness and Coach Seville's compliment, Angel didn't seem particularly confident or enthusiastic.

Coach Seville's head jerked upward, and she glared toward the back of the gym.

"If I hear that again, the person who says it will be asked to leave and not be permitted to audition *at all.*" She said the last two words so firmly Jamee knew she meant business. "On this squad, we treat each other with respect. You hear me?"

"Yes," the girls mumbled.

"I'm sorry. I didn't hear you," barked the coach.

"YES!" answered the girls, much louder this time.

"That's better!" Coach Seville replied, grabbing a clipboard off the edge of the bleachers. "Now, I'm going to break you into smaller groups and give you a few more minutes to practice. And then, just to get you ready for auditions, I'm going to ask each group to perform for us. Are you ready?"

A loud "Yes, Coach" erupted from all over the room as the girls scrambled to get ready. But this time, Jamee noticed that Angel didn't join in. Instead, the skinny girl stared at her shoes as if she had never seen them before.

Jamee could hear her muttering to herself, "Left, left, right, kick, clap, slap, turn . . . left, left, right, kick, clap, slap, turn" repeating the order of the steps to herself like a chant. It was sort of weird.

Coach Seville then counted them off. Jamee, Amberlynn, and Angel were assigned to different groups. Jamee forgot all about the strange girl as she practiced the routine with her group. They stumbled a bit, but by the time Coach Seville boomed out "Time's up!" she was pretty sure she wouldn't embarrass herself in front of the other girls.

"Group one, front and center, please!"

A line of girls rose from the bleachers, including Angel and Tasha's new friend Vanessa.

"Go home," Vanessa muttered to Angel as she strutted past her onto the gym floor. Jamee looked up in surprise. She glanced at Coach Seville, who didn't seem to hear Vanessa's comment.

Angel looked as if she had been slapped.

"Crystal's going to count off," Coach Seville told them. "Then you start. Ready?"

"Ready!" the girls in the group shouted back, sounding like a military drill team saluting their general.

Crystal counted off and they started. Most of the girls had the opening of the cheer down, but there were a couple who messed up from the first sequence.

"And break!" they chanted, moving into the step routine.

Jamee watched as everything fell apart. She was surprised to see how messy the girls looked. Most didn't seem to remember the steps, and two of the girls just stopped halfway through. The only two girls who did anything close to the routine were Vanessa . . . and Angel. Vanessa did everything so perfectly it was as if she had made it up herself. She even tossed her hair and swung her hips and smiled as if she was selling something. Jamee had to give it to her. The girl could move.

But to Jamee's surprise, Angel could, too. She stepped left instead of right twice and bumped into the girl next to her once. But that didn't matter because she recovered immediately and kept going, with her head down and her eyes locked on her feet. She didn't look up at all—not even long enough to see how much the other girls were messing up. When the sequence ended, the girls on the bleachers clapped politely.

"Thank you, ladies. Some of you have a lot of work to do before Thursday. And almost all of you need to find your smile. Even when you mess up, you should be smiling," Coach Seville said. "Let's go, group two."

Vanessa strolled off the floor with a big grin on her face. Tasha nearly fell out of the bleachers to congratulate her. Jamee didn't like watching it. Besides, Amberlynn's group was up next. She crossed her fingers for her friend as Crystal called out.

"Ready? Three, two, one . . . let's go!" and the group began their cheer.

Amberlynn did pretty well. Like Vanessa, she kept her head up with a big smile on her face as Coach Seville said, even though she messed up a few times. Then Jamee's group got called.

Jamee gave it all she had, pushing

away Mrs. Guessner and her algebra test and the gnawing feeling that she was making a mistake. Instead, she kept her head up with a smile on her face, and she pushed.

When the step routine began, she heard a strange voice in the back of her mind, like a chant.

"Left, left, right, kick, clap, slap, turn." It was Angel's, and it helped.

When she finished, Jamee was sweating, but she knew she hadn't missed a single step.

"That was great!" Amberlynn said, squeezing Jamee's shoulder. "Actually, it was perfect! How'd you memorize it so fast?"

"It wasn't me really," Jamee began. "It was—"

"That's all for today, everyone!" Coach Seville's loud voice interrupted her. "See you here tomorrow, same time."

Jamee and Amberlynn stood up with the other girls and filed out of the gym. Jamee took a quick look around for Angel McAllister. She almost wanted to thank her.

But the odd girl was already gone.

Chapter 3

"Yo, Jamee," Desmond Hodden yelled as she came out of the building. "It's about time, girl. I was about to come into that gym and get you myself."

"Yeah, right," Jamee said with a smile as he approached. "Coach Seville woulda kicked your butt all over the gym if you'd stepped foot in there."

"You're probably right. That woman's fierce!" Dez said before giving her a sloppy kiss.

Jamee had been seeing Dez all summer. He was the nicest boy she had ever hung out with, even though Darcy thought they kissed too much. *So what?* Jamee figured. Darcy wasn't Mom, and Jamee wasn't about to let her sister tell her how to be with boys. Forget that.

"Dang, J!" he cried, looking at the

clothes she wore to cheerleading practice. "These shorts are short!" He
grinned and then broke into some lines
of a popular song.

*Baby got a booty; it's workin' double
    duty*
*Fillin' out her jeans, she's my little
    cutie—*

"Stop it, Dez!" Jamee yelled, suddenly feeling embarrassed. Many of the
girls from tryouts were hanging around
in front of the school, and Dez's singing
had gotten their attention. Some were
staring at them. Jamee cringed inside
and started walking.

"Hey, it's just a song," Dez laughed
as he fell into step beside her. "I was just
messin' around, that's all. Besides, you
look *good*. Why can't I speak the truth?
It's what guys do with their girlfriends,
right?" He dropped an arm over her
shoulder.

"That's not the point," Jamee said.
She wanted to get away from the front of
the school where everyone could hear
them.

"Hey, Jamee! Hold up!"

Jamee turned. Tasha Jenkins was
behind them, along with Vanessa Pierce

and a couple of other girls Jamee didn't know.

Dez's arm dropped off Jamee's shoulder as the girls approached.

Even though Tasha had also gone to Irving Middle School, Jamee never really considered her a friend. There was always something a bit fake about her that kept Jamee from getting too close. Tasha's smile always seemed to be just a little too big, or her eyes just a little too curious, even now as she walked closer.

"I want you to meet some people. Jamee, this is Vanessa." Tasha sounded as if she was introducing them to royalty. "And her friends Renita and Kym. This is Jamee. And her boyfriend, Desmond."

Vanessa looked Jamee over as if she was inspecting something.

"You were good, Jamee. You'll probably make the squad unless you screw up big time on Thursday," she said confidently. "Trust me. I've been through this before. Last year, I knew the first day who was going to make it and who wasn't." She flipped her head and made her long hair fly.

Up close, Jamee was sure Vanessa's hair wasn't real, but it still looked nice.

And with her curvy hips and her chest filling her T-shirt, Vanessa seemed like the kind of girl you would see in a magazine. Jamee suddenly felt small and almost boyish, no matter what Dez said. His eyes were on Vanessa, too.

"I would've made it last year, but I sprained my ankle doing a roundoff and had to sit out while it healed," she explained. "But from what I've seen, I think you're good enough to make it."

"Thanks," Jamee replied, almost blushing. There was something about being praised by Vanessa that made her feel as if she had already made the cheerleading squad.

"But I have to say, some of these girls were just a *mess*," Vanessa continued, her face scrunching as if she saw something that disgusted her. "You know, the ones stepping on people's toes? Mumbling the steps to themselves? The ones who can't even cheer and smile at the same time?" She rolled her eyes. "We don't need no clumsy girls embarrassing us, do we?"

"No way," Renita agreed. She was lighter-skinned, with curly hair that framed her face. "People will laugh us off the field when we play Zamora. We can't have that."

Though no one said it, Jamee knew they were talking about Angel. She felt awkward talking about the girl behind her back.

"I saw you, Jamee. You got stepped on, like, a million times," Vanessa said sympathetically. "Seriously, I felt bad for you."

"It wasn't *that* bad," Jamee said, trying to change the subject. "I mean, everyone was messin' up at first." She knew she wasn't telling the whole truth. Angel had been really uncoordinated in the beginning. And her foot still hurt from where the girl had stomped it.

"I'm sorry, but that girl Angel was the *worst,*" Kym cut in. She had brown skin and wore her hair pulled back in a smooth black bun. "Did you see the look on her face while she was doing the routine?" she asked. Then she scrunched her face into a tight frown, imitating Angel. "She looked retarded or something."

Tasha cackled loudly. Too loudly, Jamee thought.

"That's funny!" she cried, clapping her hands. "Retarded. That's exactly what she looked like!" Tasha crossed her eyes and twisted her lips, making her face distorted and ugly. "Go Bluford!" she yelled, her voice loud and unnatural, mocking the way Angel yelled out during practice.

The older girls laughed and Tasha beamed with pride.

Dez didn't say anything. Jamee knew he didn't like that kind of talk either, but his eyes were fixed on Vanessa's T-shirt.

"Speak of the devil," Renita muttered, cocking her head.

Jamee turned, along with the rest of the girls, to see Angel walking along the sidewalk alone with her head down and a heavy-looking backpack on her shoulders.

"She still looks retarded, if you ask me," mumbled Kym. The rest of the girls chuckled.

Angel seemed to hear the laughter. She looked up and noticed the girls watching her. Immediately her eyes locked on her feet as if some invisible chain held them down.

"You know, *some people* don't have what it takes for cheerleading," Vanessa said loudly as Angel got closer. "I'm not sure why *some people* even bothered to try out."

"Mmm hmm," Kym said in agreement. "I don't know neither."

Vanessa turned to face Angel as she approached. "I know *some people* better not step on *my* foot. I've spent too much money on my sneakers to have somebody scuffing them up with their stinky old shoes."

"I bet her shoes do stink," Tasha added. Again the girls laughed.

Jamee squirmed. She hated what Vanessa was doing. She could see by the worried look on Angel's face that she was scared. Jamee knew if she remained quiet, Angel would think she was just like Vanessa and the rest of her mean friends. Jamee didn't want that. And yet if she stood up for Angel, Jamee knew she could get into trouble. Vanessa and her friends might turn on her. That was the last thing she needed: a bunch of upperclass girls as enemies. Still, she couldn't just sit there and do nothing.

"Yeah, but if Angel moves like she did in the second routine, she probably ain't gonna step on anyone's shoes again," Jamee said, hoping to let Angel know she was on her side.

Vanessa and Kym glanced at her. Angel didn't say a word. She just kept her head down and walked a little faster, as if ignoring the girls was the best way to deal with them. Jamee couldn't blame her. She wished the sidewalk were wider and Angel didn't have to get so close to them.

"Yeah, well, you gotta have the whole package to be a cheerleader," Tasha chimed in. Angel was only two car-lengths away. "And it helps if you're good-looking," she said with a frown. "But since she ain't got no hope for that, she better at least learn the moves."

Renita and Kym hooted at Tasha's comment, raising their hands to their mouths as ugly laughter spilled through their fingers. Finally Dez seemed to wake up.

"That was cold, Tasha," he muttered, shaking his head. "Why you wanna say a thing like that?"

"'Cause it's true," Vanessa replied. The girls laughed even louder.

Angel ignored them. She made a move to rush by the group, but Vanessa stuck out her foot. Angel tripped, hitting the sidewalk on all fours. Her books tumbled from her backpack as she fell. Jamee could see she scraped her leg.

"Hey!" Dez protested. He bent over

her, stretching out his hand to help her. "You okay?"

Angel ignored him. She bounded to her feet as if she wasn't hurt, even though a raw red mark appeared just below her knee.

"How is she gonna be a cheerleader? This girl can't even walk straight." Vanessa shook her head and smirked. Angel quickly stooped to gather her books.

"I saw you trip her," Jamee muttered. "Why did you do that?"

Kym rolled her eyes as if what Jamee said bothered her. "Aren't you Darcy Wills's sister?"

"Yeah, so?"

"Well, I guess I thought you'd be smarter," Kym replied with an edge to her voice.

Just then, a burst of electronic music sliced into the air. Tasha pulled a pink cell phone out of her purse and flipped it open. Angel quickly grabbed the last of her books and rushed off without a word. Jamee wanted to follow her, but she couldn't bring herself to leave the group of girls. Instead she watched Angel wander down the street alone.

"I *told* you I had cheerleading, Mom,"

Tasha said impatiently into the phone. "Don't you remember? I said it, like, a hundred times," she spoke in a tone Jamee wouldn't dare use with Mom. And yet, Jamee thought, it almost sounded as if Tasha was putting on a performance. "Okay. Fine," she said finally and hung up.

Vanessa continued as if the phone never rang. "I didn't trip her, Jamee," she said sweetly. "I moved at the same time she did, that's all. It ain't my fault if she gets tangled up in her own feet, is it?" Vanessa blinked innocently. "Besides, be real, Jamee. Do you really think she belongs out there with us?"

Jamee paused. She didn't like the way Vanessa, Tasha, and their friends were acting, but she knew Angel *was* a little odd. Not like the kind of girl who would really fit in.

"See," Tasha sounded triumphant. "You *know* she's a hot mess, Jamee. So just keep your mouth shut and leave it to Vanessa. She knows how to handle girls like her. Don't you, Vanessa?"

"Thanks, Tasha." Vanessa put her arms around Tasha's shoulders and gave her a quick squeeze. "You're like the little sister I never had, you know that? Oh, by the way, could I have your phone for a second?"

Tasha stared at her phone. For an instant she was frozen, as if she didn't know what to do. "Well . . . my mom said I wasn't supposed to . . ."

Vanessa's arm slid off Tasha's back. "Oh," she said coldly. "Well. I just wanted to text my mom at work and let her know I was on my way home. But that's okay. Maybe I'll find someone *else* who's willing to help me—"

"No, no! It's all right if it's just for a second." Tasha fished the phone out of her bag and handed it over. "But just one quick text, okay?"

A wide grin stretched across Vanessa's face. "Thanks, girl. You're the best." She looked the phone over, touching the buttons. "Can you take pictures with this, too?"

"Pictures, movies," Tasha answered, beaming with pride. "I saved all summer to buy it, but Mom said I can only have a few minutes a month and when they're all gone I don't get anymore," she added as Vanessa's long fingernails tapped the keyboard.

"I understand," Vanessa said, pressing *Send.* "Thanks, girl. You're all right.

Let's go to my house. We can practice our jumps for tomorrow." Her eyes flicked over Jamee. "You can come, too, Jamee." She then smiled at Dez as if she knew something Jamee didn't. "Unless you guys have other plans . . ."

"Thanks, but I have to go home," Jamee said quickly. "I'm already late. We're going to dinner at my aunt's house." It sounded like a lie, but it wasn't. Jamee dreaded seeing Aunt Charlotte. Like the algebra test, it was something she had been doing her best to forget about all day. "I have to go home and change."

Vanessa flipped her hair extensions and smiled. "Well, I guess we have lots of time to practice and get to know each other. I'm telling you right now, this is half the new cheerleaders, standing right *here!*" She squeezed Tasha's shoulder again and they walked off, with Renita and Kym following less than a step behind.

Jamee hoped what Vanessa said was true, that she would make the squad. But she was still bothered by what happened with Angel.

And Kym's comment.

And the way Tasha seemed so fake,

especially around Vanessa.

"Man, them girls are *mean*. Like a pack of dogs, only better looking," Dez joked.

"Yeah, I noticed you couldn't keep your eyes off Vanessa. Maybe you're a dog, too."

"C'mon, J. My eyes were on you most of the time, but you didn't notice," he said defensively. "Hey, Cooper said he'd treat for pizza tomorrow after school. Wanna come?"

Jamee hesitated. She knew Darcy would probably be there, too, since she was best friends with Cooper and his girlfriend, Tarah. The last thing Jamee wanted to do was hang out with her sister when she didn't have to.

"I got cheerleading, Dez. I don't know—"

"So come late," he interrupted.

"All right. Maybe after practice."

"Cool." Dez looked over his shoulder, then leaned in and gave Jamee a long, lingering kiss on the lips that left her a little breathless.

"Tomorrow," he said. "Don't forget."

"You're late," Darcy barked as soon as Jamee walked in the door.

39

"You're not my mother, Darcy," Jamee snapped. "You're only two years older than me. I don't know why you think you can talk to me like you're my boss or something." Jamee slapped her books on the kitchen chair, grabbed a glass and filled it with water. After two weeks of hearing each teacher at Bluford tell her she was dumber than Darcy, the last thing Jamee wanted was a lecture from her.

Darcy frowned. "Well, everyone else is almost ready, and you know how important this is to Mom—"

"I know, Darcy. I don't need you to tell me, okay?"

"Then why are you so late?"

"I told you this morning," Jamee said between gulps of water. "It was the first day of cheerleading tryouts. Remember?"

Darcy grunted. She sat at the kitchen table wearing khaki pants and a white blouse. Textbooks were spread around her at the table. In addition, there were a couple of thick library books stacked right in front of her. *The Official SAT Study Guide* was on top. Darcy was only a junior at Bluford, but lately all she talked about was "college this" and "college that." Mom and Dad were no better. When they weren't talking about the new baby, there were nonstop discussions about Darcy getting a scholarship if her SAT scores were high enough.

She's only a junior, Jamee wanted to scream each time the subject came up. *And it's only September. Why's everybody rushing everything?* Last week Jamee mentioned it to her sister, and Darcy snapped.

"Just because you *blow off school doesn't mean I'm going to,"* Darcy had yelled. Mom jumped in on Darcy's side. Jamee rolled her eyes at them. She was still angry that they ganged up on her.

"So how were the tryouts?" Darcy mumbled as she flipped through the SAT book.

"Fine," Jamee muttered. She would have liked to tell her about how hard the step routine was or what had gone down with Vanessa and Tasha and that odd girl Angel. But she could see Darcy wasn't interested. Her eyes were focused on the page in front of her.

"Is Dad here yet?" Jamee asked.

Dad had struggled to find work since Mom announced she was pregnant. Recently, he took a new day-job as a customer service representative for the cable company. At night, he was a cab driver. Most evenings, he barely had enough time to eat dinner before heading out to work again.

Darcy nodded. "He and Mom are getting ready. You really should hurry up and get changed. If we're late to Aunt Charlotte's because of you, Mom's gonna get upset. You remember what her doctor said—"

"Jamee?" Mom's angry voice cut Darcy off. She stood in the hallway in a blue dress stretched tight around her pregnant belly. "Why aren't you ready? We're supposed to be at Charlotte's in half an hour!"

"I told you," Darcy mumbled under her breath.

"I can get ready in five minutes, Mom," Jamee said, moving toward her room.

Mom had been tired and irritable for weeks. Last month, she was so exhausted that her back had given out one night at work at the hospital. Her doctors explained that the pregnancy and the long hours as an ER nurse were too much for her forty-year-old body. The family had talked about it and agreed to help out more so Mom wouldn't be so stressed.

But then Aunt Charlotte called and invited the family to dinner. Jamee thought it was a bad idea from the start. Mom always seemed tense around her sister. And Jamee couldn't stand to go to her house since a fight they had there last year. Yet for some reason, Mom agreed to go.

"You were supposed to be home by 4:30," her mother fussed as Jamee walked down the hallway. "What were you doing all that time?"

"Cheerleading tryouts!" Jamee cried. "I told you yesterday, remember?" She was used to repeating herself. No one in the house seemed to listen to a word she said.

Her mother took a deep breath. "I told you I'm not sure about you cheering right now, Jamee," she grumbled. "You barely made it out of eighth grade, and that counselor said you need to pay attention to your schoolwork."

"Yeah, I know what he said," Jamee grumbled, thinking of Mrs. Guessner and the crumpled test somewhere at the bottom of her backpack. She didn't know how she would ever get her parents to sign it.

"Since I'm late, maybe you should

just go on without me," she offered. "Aunt Charlotte hates me anyway."

Mom glared at her. "Don't start with me, Jamee Wills," Mom said. Whenever her mother used her last name, Jamee knew she was getting mad.

"You two may not always see eye to eye, but she still loves you. Understand?" Mom stared hard into Jamee's face.

Jamee knew better than to say anything. Instead she nodded.

"You're going, and you'll be nice," Mom added.

"I'll try. But what am I supposed to do when *she*'s not nice? What if she acts the way she did last time when she started saying mean things about me— and about Dad? I can't stand sittin' there while she's badmouthin' and lookin' down on us."

"No matter what she says, you'll mind your place, you hear me?" Mom warned. "She's your aunt and you'll show her respect."

Jamee could see the lines in her mother's forehead and the weariness in her eyes. She knew she should just stop arguing with her, but in that moment she just couldn't.

"So I'm supposed to just sit in her

stupid dining room while she disrespects me?"

"YES!" Dad boomed from down the hallway. "You heard your mother, and you know better than to keep arguing with her, especially right now."

"Just drop it, Jamee," Darcy added from the dining room.

Jamee's head began to throb. She wanted to scream at everyone in the house. None of them seemed to listen or care about her anymore. Everything was focused on the baby or Mom's health or Darcy's SAT scores. Nothing else mattered. For an instant, Jamee could feel angry tears in her eyes. Mom seemed to notice them.

"Please, Jamee," she said calmly. "Just go and get ready. For my sake, if for no other reason."

Jamee took a deep breath, fighting to swallow down her rage.

"Fine," she said sullenly. She grabbed her backpack and hurried to her room, slamming the door.

Chapter 4

"So," Aunt Charlotte said, eyeing Jamee from her seat at the head of her fancy wooden table. "What's new with you?"

Jamee shrugged. She had hoped Aunt Charlotte would just ignore her for the entire meal. So far it had worked. Jamee had quietly smeared the goopy vegetable lasagna around her plate, pretending to eat it just to be polite.

"*That's all organic vegetables. Mushrooms, eggplant, and squash,*" Aunt Charlotte boasted several times since they sat down. "*I know you probably don't get good produce where you live, so I figured I'd get some for you.*"

Darcy had thanked her, but Jamee fumed as she stared at the mushy mixture. *It's not like we live that far away*

46

from you, she wanted to say. *Why do you always act like you're better than us? Besides,* she almost said out loud, *it may be organic or whatever, but it's still nasty.*

Every time Jamee visited Aunt Charlotte, it was the same—food that made her want to gag and comments that made her want to scream.

It was as if everything her aunt said had an edge to it, like each word was an invisible knife aimed at Jamee and her family. While they were never direct, Aunt Charlotte's comments were full of jabs about Dad's job or Mom's tired face or their neighborhood being an unfit place to raise a baby. The last time Jamee visited, she couldn't hold her thoughts back. Instead she accused her aunt of being selfish and mean. That's when Aunt Charlotte told her to get out and never to come back.

Jamee was fine with the idea, but then Aunt Charlotte called last week and invited them over. Maybe she realized that with Grandma gone, they were the only family she had left in the world. Or maybe it was something else. Jamee couldn't help but wonder what Aunt Charlotte really wanted.

"*Jamee*," Mom's voice was full of warning, breaking her thoughts. "Aunt Charlotte just asked you a question."

Jamee sat up in her chair, trying her best to stay calm. "Nothing really. I just started at Bluford. I'm still getting used to it. New teachers and classes, you know. It's really different from middle school."

"Yes, it's very different from middle school. And I hope you're gonna treat it differently, too. Like Darcy."

Anger churned in Jamee's stomach, but she pressed her lips together and said nothing.

"Don't worry, Charlotte. Jamee knows what she's gotta do," Mom said icily.

Aunt Charlotte put a forkful of lasagna into her mouth, and for a second an awkward silence filled the room.

"Well, I hope so. I'd like to see her go to college one day too, you know. That's what this is all about, right?"

Again silence filled the room. Jamee felt like dumping her plate of lasagna on the beige carpeted floor and walking home. Instead she took a sip of water from the oversized glass and tried to hide that her hand was shaking with anger. Dad seemed to notice because he put his hand gently on her back, as if it would steady her somehow.

"Jamee'll get there when she's ready. I have no doubt of that," Dad said.

Aunt Charlotte ignored his comment. She stood up suddenly, as if the dinner had reached a point she had been expecting.

"Well, I was going to wait until after dessert, but since we're talking about college, I think now's as good a time as any to make this announcement." She beamed from the head of the table, stopping for a second to smile at Darcy.

"I've bought you all something. A gift, I guess." She disappeared into the kitchen and returned a few seconds later with a big box topped with a red bow. She plopped it on Darcy's lap.

"Go on. Open it," she urged, not once looking at Jamee.

Darcy glanced at her parents and then pulled at the ribbon carefully, loosening the paper as if the contents were delicate. Jamee wished Aunt Charlotte had given her the box to open. She would have torn through it in seconds.

When the paper was finally gone, Jamee saw the picture on the box. *Could it be? No, people reuse boxes*, she told

49

herself. *Would Aunt Charlotte be that generous?*

Darcy opened the cardboard. "Oh, Aunt Charlotte!" she cried, lifting a brand new laptop computer out of the box. "Are you serious?!"

A computer! Jamee couldn't believe it either.

"Of course I'm serious! And it's for you, Darcy," Aunt Charlotte said with a wide grin. "For *all* of you really, but I figured it might help now that Darcy is getting ready for college. These days a student who doesn't have regular access to the Internet can't compete! And I figured, Mattie, you could research the latest on childcare. Carl, maybe you can take some online classes so you can find a better job or something."

Her father blinked. His mouth stretched into a tight forced smile, but he said nothing.

"And Jamee, well, maybe when you're serious it'll help you improve your grades, too," she added, as if she only half believed what she was saying.

You can keep your stupid computer and your nasty lasagna. Jamee almost yelled the words right there at the table. Mom must have noticed because she flashed Jamee a glare that froze her in her seat. Instead Jamee pushed her plate away and leaned over the table to look at the silvery screen sitting on Darcy's lap.

Jamee had wanted a computer for a long time, but not as a gift from Aunt Charlotte. She would rather use the computers at school or the library or her friend Alisha Wrobel's house than give her aunt another reason to act as if she was better than them.

"I don't know what to say," Mom began. "Charlotte, this is very generous of you, but we can't accept this—"

"Mattie," Aunt Charlotte's voice grew sharp. "Don't you even think of letting that misplaced pride of yours get in the way. These girls *need* a computer, and I'm giving it to them and that's that."

Mom glanced at Dad. She looked as if she wanted him to decide, as if she already had too much to think about.

Give it back, Jamee nearly yelled out. *We don't need no handouts from her.* But Darcy was busy touching the keys as if they were precious.

"Tell her, Carl," Aunt Charlotte said. "You know this is good for your girls."

Dad didn't move. For a second,

Jamee thought he was going to refuse the computer, but then he looked at Darcy and sighed. "Thank you, Charlotte," he said finally, as if admitting defeat. "We've wanted to get the girls a computer for a while now, but with bills and the baby coming . . ." he shook his head. "We really could use this."

"Good. So it's settled then." Aunt Charlotte smiled as if she had won an argument. "The software's loaded already. All you'll need is an Internet connection."

"We'll take care of that, Charlotte. It's very generous. Thank you," Mom said.

Aunt Charlotte folded her arms across her chest. "Go on. Turn it on, Darcy. You can plug it into the living room outlet. You should have no trouble getting online."

Darcy dashed away from the dinner table and Jamee followed just to get away from her aunt. Within minutes the computer was connected.

"Check out SpaceBook or MyFace," Jamee suggested. "Or go to UTube." Anything was better than just sitting in her aunt's stuffy living room.

"In a minute, Jamee," Darcy said. She sat in front of the screen and started typing. "There's something I want to check out first."

Mom sat down on the sofa beside Darcy, and Aunt Charlotte hovered over Darcy's shoulder while she typed. A few moments later, the website for UCLA popped up.

"It's very competitive," Aunt Charlotte said. "But they have some amazing scholarship programs. With your grades, you have a decent shot. But you'll need good SAT scores, too."

Aunt Charlotte wedged herself onto the sofa beside Darcy, nudging Jamee out of the way as she spoke.

"I know. I've been studying for weeks," Darcy said.

Aunt Charlotte nodded. "Excellent. Keep at it. If you can do well on that test and hold your grades, I think you'll qualify."

"You really think so, Charlotte?" Mom sounded both nervous and excited at the same time.

"Absolutely. Who wouldn't want a student like Darcy in their school?" Aunt Charlotte asked.

Then they all started talking about colleges. The computer screen filled with images of schools and programs and

53

financial aid forms.

She's still got two years! Jamee wanted to say, but it didn't matter.

Jamee never even got to touch the keyboard. For the rest of the evening, she sat in a chair at the corner of the room while Aunt Charlotte and her parents talked about Darcy's future as though it was the only one that mattered.

"Jamee, do you have something for me?"

Mrs. Guessner stretched out her hand.

Jamee had tried all morning to think of an excuse for her teacher. The truth was she couldn't bring herself to show her parents the test, not after the way Mom scolded her about cheerleading, not after the dinner with Aunt Charlotte.

"I'm sorry. I forgot it, Mrs. Guessner. I left it on the kitchen counter at home. My mom signed it, but I was in a rush this morning, and I didn't put it in my backpack."

It was partly true at least. She did forget it, and she was late this morning. But Mrs. Guessner didn't seem convinced. "You didn't show up for after-school help yesterday, either," she said sternly.

"I know, but I told you. It's cheer-leading tryouts."

Mrs. Guessner opened her mouth, and Jamee knew she was going to repeat what she had said the day before about cheering and good grades. She didn't want to hear it.

"But I got my sister to help me with it when I got home," she added quickly.

Mrs. Guessner's mouth closed and her expression changed. "Well," she said at last. "I'm glad to hear that. As I told you yesterday, it's very important that . . ."

She kept talking, and Jamee tried to listen. But as her teacher's voice droned on, Jamee kept imagining Friday and how good it would feel to look up at the bulletin board and see her name as one of the new cheerleaders. Now was the time to focus on making the squad, she figured. She could deal with her algebra grades later.

"Jamee? Are you listening?"

Mrs. Guessner's sharp voice focused her back in the moment.

"Yes, ma'am," she said quickly, even though she had no idea what the woman had just said.

"Bring in that signature. If you don't,

I'm going to have to call your parents—"

"I'll bring it in tomorrow," Jamee said, nodding. "I promise."

"And I'll see you after school today?"

"Uh . . ." Jamee hesitated. "Yeah, sure."

Mrs. Guessner's face said she didn't believe her, but the students in her next class were already coming in. "Go," she said, waving her hand. "I'll see you this afternoon."

"Can I sit with you, Jamee?"

Angel stood over her with her lunch tray in her hand. Jamee was surprised, but she tried to hide it. She hadn't seen Angel in the cafeteria before.

"Sure," she said. "I didn't know we had the same lunch period. Where do you usually sit?" Jamee asked.

"Oh, wherever," Angel said, nervously looking at her plate in a way that told Jamee not to push the subject.

"Well, have a seat," Jamee said, glancing at Angel's wide-rimmed glasses and noticing how they seemed a bit too big for her face. "I can't believe I never noticed you in here before. I woulda asked you to sit here if I'd seen you."

"Yeah, well, this is a big school,"

Angel said almost sadly. "It's easy to disappear in here. Not like my old school."

"Where'd you go before?"

"Mary Bethune Academy."

"Mary Bethune Academy?" Jamee asked. She had never heard the name. "What's that?"

"It's a charter school on the other side of town. Girls only."

"*Girls only?* For real? I don't think I'd survive in a place like that," she said with a laugh. "Seriously, wasn't it weird? Goin' to a school with no boys?"

Angel shrugged. "It was okay. You get used to it. Actually, I kinda miss it now," she admitted, gently forking some spaghetti into her mouth.

"Why did you leave?"

Angel pushed her glasses back up her nose and turned the spaghetti noodles on her plate. "My parents split up," she said simply and filled her mouth with food, her eyes never meeting Jamee's. "Me, my sister, and my mom moved out this summer. She started working at Essentials Salon, and now I go to Bluford." Her voice sounded slightly higher than before, as if the words were painful to say.

Jamee remembered how hard it was

when Dad left and their family was shattered. She wondered if Angel was feeling the same way, but she didn't want to ask her. She had known her for only a day.

"Did you used to cheer at your old school?" Jamee asked instead.

Angel shook her head. "No. We didn't have cheerleading, but we did have a step team. I was an alternate last year. I might have made the team this year, if things had been different . . ." She sounded suddenly sad. Jamee tried to change the subject.

"Is that where you learned to chant out the steps?"

Angel looked confused.

"You know," Jamee explained. "Right, right, left, kick, slap, clap, stomp—"

"Oh, you heard that?" Angel laughed. "Yeah, that's how they taught the routines there. Sorry if it bothered you—"

"No," Jamee shook her head. "It kinda helped me—"

"Oh, you *gotta* be kidding me," a voice rang out behind them. Jamee turned to see Vanessa. She stood over Angel's shoulder with Kym and Renita on either side of her. Each of them held a tray with plates half-full of spaghetti. For an instant, Jamee wondered if they were going to dump them on Angel.

"So you two are eatin' lunch together now?" Kym asked as if she were disgusted.

"So what, Kym?" Jamee asked. The older girl rolled her eyes.

"We'd join you, but our friends are sitting over there." Vanessa tossed her hair toward a table full of girls dressed in jeans and tight T-shirts.

As soon as Jamee and Angel looked in their direction, the table erupted in laughter. Jamee had no idea what they were saying, but she knew it was mean. Angel knew it, too. Jamee noticed that Angel seemed to shrink inside herself. She looked as nervous and scared as when Jamee had seen her for the first time.

"You all ready for today?" Jamee asked, trying to change the subject.

"We're ready. I think the bigger question is, are *you* ready? Whatcha think, Angel? You gonna show us more of them foot stompin' moves from yesterday?" Vanessa asked.

"No, she's gonna be like '*I'm ready, Coach*'," yelled Kym, blaring out the last few words in a mock imitation of Angel's voice from the day before.

Kym and Renita burst out laughing as Angel's face sank. Jamee thought the skinny girl was about to cry, but instead, she stood up and gathered her tray.

"See you, Jamee," Angel said softly and walked away.

Jamee stood up and watched her go, feeling guilty as Angel rushed out the cafeteria door.

"See you in a few hours, Angel!" Vanessa added sweetly, though her voice meant the opposite.

"What did you do that for, Vanessa?" Jamee asked, staring hard into the older girl's heavily made-up face.

"Relax, girl. We're just playin' with her, that's all," Vanessa replied innocently. "Why you sounding like Darcy all of a sudden?" she asked, shaking her hair.

"What do you mean?"

"Look, Jamee. Everyone knows Darcy is all into school and whatever," Vanessa said as if what she described was beneath her. "But I always heard you were different, the kind of girl who knows how to hang. You're not like Darcy, who stays inside and skips parties to do her homework. You're for *real*, hookin' up with Bobby Wallace and all last year. That's serious!"

It sounded to Jamee as if Vanessa was insulting her and complimenting her at the same time.

"What do you know about me and Bobby Wallace? And my sister?"

Vanessa just laughed. "C'mon, girl. Wake up. You're in high school now. Everybody knows about you and Bobby Wallace. And that whole running away thing. And how you hooked up with Dez on the Fourth of July."

"Yeah, I heard she was makin' her own fireworks with Dez that night," added Kym.

"See?" Vanessa asked with a wicked smile. "Girl, you got a serious reputation for a freshman. That's *nothing* like your sister. I mean I heard she barely let Hakeem Randall hold her hand, right?" She chuckled a little as she glanced at her friends.

"What are you trying to say?" Jamee asked, suddenly protective of her sister.

Vanessa shook her head as if Jamee had asked her a stupid question. "I'm sayin', don't act like you're all perfect, Jamee. You ain't no better than the rest of us. Maybe you're even a little worse."

RING!

The bell announcing the end of the lunch period blasted overhead. Vanessa and her friends turned away and headed toward the door.

"See you at tryouts!" Vanessa added. Her voice almost sounded friendly, but Jamee knew not to trust it.

For the rest of the day, Jamee couldn't quite shake what Vanessa had said at lunch. It was bad enough the way she had treated Angel, but Vanessa seemed to be doing something else, too.

What did she mean about me? Jamee asked herself. *What was she trying to say?*

Jamee wasn't sure. Nothing Vanessa said was a lie. She *had* kissed Dez at the Fourth of July cookout last summer, and she *had* gone out with Bobby Wallace last year. But Vanessa made it all seem worse. Did Jamee really have a reputation at Bluford? Was it as bad as Vanessa said it was? While she didn't want to be like Darcy, she didn't want to be what Vanessa suggested, either.

"Hey, Jamee!" Dez yelled from across the hallway at the end of the day. Jamee was heading to tryouts when he walked up beside her, dropped his heavy arm on her shoulder and leaned in for a kiss. Jamee turned her head just in time so his lips pressed against her cheek.

"What's the matter?" Dez asked. He looked hurt and surprised at the same time.

"Nothing . . . I just . . ." she shrugged, shifting away from him slightly. "Everyone's looking at us."

Dez glanced over his shoulder. The hall was almost empty. The few students near them were rushing to their lockers or darting into classrooms. Jamee realized that no one seemed to be looking at them, but she still felt they were.

"Since when did you care 'bout that?"

Jamee looked up at Dez. He was taller than most of the freshman boys and not bad looking, with dark brown skin, deep brown eyes and white teeth. Jamee knew most girls thought he was handsome, but with Vanessa's words still in her mind, she didn't feel lucky to be his girl right now.

"I'm late for cheerleading, okay?" She started walking more quickly. Unsettled by Vanessa's comments, Jamee realized that she had forgotten to take the back hall toward the locker room. Instead she was near the front of the school and would pass Mrs. Guessner's classroom. She knew she could turn around, but that would make her late, and she would have to explain it all to Dez. Instead, she hoped she could rush past Mrs. Guessner's classroom without the algebra teacher seeing her.

"I'm sorry. I guess I'm just nervous," she said. It was true, but Jamee knew that wasn't the only thing she was thinking. Vanessa had made her feel strange about Dez in ways she couldn't explain to him, at least not now.

Dez rolled his eyes at her comment. "Nervous? C'mon, Jamee. You know you're gonna make it. At least, *I* know you are. And after you're done, we goin' to the park, right?"

Jamee sighed. She didn't feel like hanging out, but she couldn't think of an excuse.

"Okay," she agreed. "But just for a little while."

Dez gave her a bright smile and leaned down to kiss her again. Jamee let him peck her once on the lips, then pulled away.

"Jamee?" Dez asked, looking puzzled. "What's up?"

You got a serious reputation for a freshman. Vanessa's words taunted her.

"Nothing. I just have to go," Jamee said. Now wasn't the time to talk to Dez about all that. "See you at the park."

She walked quickly down the hall, scuttling past Mrs. Guessner's room. She thought she was safe until she looked back over her shoulder. Mrs. Guessner had just stepped into the hallway. Her eyes locked on Jamee's but instead of calling her into the classroom, the teacher just shook her head and closed the door.

The locker room was quieter than yesterday. Jamee could feel the tension in the air. It was as if the reality of how much they all had to learn and remember had settled over everyone. Jamee looked around. There weren't as many girls, either. Some had already dropped out.

Amberlynn smiled when Jamee eased past her but kept her focus on tightly tying her shoelaces. Jamee didn't feel like talking anyway. Her mind was swirling with thoughts about Vanessa and Angel, about what she wanted to say to Dez when they were finally alone, about the way Mrs. Guessner shook her head as if Jamee was a lost cause, about home and how she felt increasingly like an outsider there.

"Stop it! Come on! Give it back!"

The cries interrupted Jamee's thoughts. Something was happening in the next row of lockers. The girls involved were hidden from view, but Jamee thought she recognized the voices.

"What's that all about?" Amberlynn murmured, crinkling her brow.

"Stop it! Stop it!" the girl in the next row yelled again. Jamee put on her shorts and hurried to see what was going on.

Angel stood in between the two rows of lockers, wearing her jeans and her sports bra while her T-shirt flew in the air between Renita and Vanessa. Tasha held her little pink phone upward, following the action like the director of a movie. Kym and a few of the other girls cheered their game of monkey-in-the-middle with smiles on their faces.

"Just give it back," Angel hollered as her top flew out of reach. She looked as if she was about to cry.

"It's not like she even needs it," Renita said. "She's so skinny and flat, she almost looks like a boy!"

"Yeah, you sure you in the right place, Angel?" Kym asked. "This is the *girls'* locker room!"

All four girls cackled loudly. Jamee couldn't stand it.

"Leave her alone!" she yelled, stepping into the crowd of girls, making sure Angel was safe behind her. "Give her back her shirt."

For an instant, the back of the locker room went silent. Yet for some reason, Vanessa smiled as if she expected Jamee to get upset.

"Girl, you need to chill. We were just playin', that's all. Why you gotta go makin' a big deal out of everything?" Vanessa spoke as if Jamee had done something wrong. She then grabbed the T-shirt from Kym. "Here," she said tossing it to Angel. "*You* know we were just playin'. Right, Angel?"

Angel stared at Vanessa. Jamee could see she was intimidated.

"Yeah," Angel mumbled. "I guess so."

Jamee could barely hear her voice.

"See?" Vanessa said, flashing Jamee a smirk. She then whispered something to Tasha and walked away.

"Are you okay?" Jamee asked. She

67

wondered how Angel would be able to handle tryouts after what just happened.

Angel nodded and wiped her eyes. "I don't know why they keep messin' with me. I didn't do anything except go to my locker," she said.

"C'mon, girl, don't worry about them right now," Jamee said, putting her arm around Angel's shoulder. "You gotta get dressed. Coach Seville will be blowing that whistle in a few minutes."

Angel nodded, gathered up her clothes, and quickly got changed.

Nearby, Tasha buried her cell phone deep in her locker as if it contained a priceless treasure. Then she rushed off without a word.

Chapter 5

"Let's go, ladies," barked Coach Seville as Jamee and Angel rushed out of the locker room.

Jamee knew they were the last ones out. She raced to the bleachers and grabbed a seat. Angel was right beside her. Even before she sat down, Jamee noticed that the gym floor was layered with thick blue mats.

"As you may have heard, gymnastics is a love of mine," Coach Seville began, pacing slowly in front of them. "And it is a useful skill in cheerleading. So I'd like to see what each of you knows today. For some of you, this might be tough, but don't worry. You don't have to have any tumbling skills to make the squad. But they certainly will help."

Tumbling skills.

The words made Jamee's heart race. Since grade school, she had always been agile and fast in gym class, especially with gymnastics. Years of cheerleading had only improved her skills. Where Darcy had a natural talent for schoolwork, Jamee knew her sister couldn't touch her with athletics. Sometimes Jamee wondered if that was why she liked sports so much. Maybe if Darcy weren't so clumsy, Jamee would never have become a cheerleader. Jamee wasn't sure. All she was certain of was that she wanted to prove to Darcy, Coach Seville, and Vanessa that she belonged on Bluford's squad.

Jamee's palms began to sweat as Coach Seville explained four popular cheerleading jumps. Jamee knew all of them, along with their strange names— the toe-touch, tuck, hurdler, and herkie. For a few minutes, Crystal and the other Varsity girls demonstrated the moves perfectly. Jamee could see by the looks on some girls' faces that the moves were new to them.

Coach Seville then called up each girl by her number to show what she could do. Tasha was one of the first, and Jamee knew she had set the bar high with the basic moves plus a back hand-spring.

"Very nice," Coach Seville said, nodding. "Good work!"

Vanessa was next. The older girl did the same basic moves but added a few nice handsprings and a back walkover. Jamee knew she was showing off, especially with the way she smiled as if she was trying to sell something.

When it was her turn, Jamee nailed the main steps. Then, with Coach Seville watching, she knew she couldn't let the other two girls show her up. She finished her jumps, dashed forward and cartwheeled across the gym floor, concentrating on keeping her arms and legs as straight as possible. When there was no more room to cartwheel, Jamee stopped, skipped a bit, then flipped head over heels, letting both feet hit the mat at the same time in a perfect roundoff.

Poom! The mat thundered when she landed. It was just what Jamee wanted.

"Whoa!" several girls cheered. Jamee made sure to look at Vanessa, who said nothing.

"Very, very nice," Coach Seville smiled and wrote quickly in her clipboard.

Amberlynn went next. She was one

of the best tumblers on the Irving Middle School squad. Jamee knew she would do well. She finished her routine with something Jamee had seen her do before: a backflip which she turned into a handstand and actually walked toward Coach Seville's seat.

"Wow!" the woman exclaimed when Amberlynn finally stood on her feet. "Very impressive! But I think all this showing off might be going a bit far, ladies." Again, she jotted in her clipboard and then called out. "Number thirty-five!"

Jamee knew it was Angel's number.

"Loser," someone croaked, covering the word with a cough.

Jamee turned her head to see who had said it. Behind her, there were several girls with guilty grins on their faces, but Vanessa had the widest smile of all. Coach Seville was glaring into the bleachers, too.

"*Ladies*," she said sternly. "You may end up being squadmates. And squadmates owe each other respect. Do I make myself clear?" When no one said anything, she said it again, "*Do I make myself clear?*"

There were some murmured "yeahs,"

and the coach stared in silence at the girls in the bleachers for a long minute. Finally she turned to Angel, who stood nervously at the edge of the mat.

"Go on, girl. Show me what you got."

Angel nodded, took a deep breath and performed a sluggish version of the four jumps the coach had requested. When she finished, she looked confused, as if she wasn't sure what to do next. Jamee squirmed inside watching her, especially after what had happened in the locker room.

"Can you do a cartwheel?" Coach Seville asked.

Angel paused and then stretched her arms and whirled around, but her cartwheel was weak. She had too little speed and nearly fell over in a heap on the floor. Jamee could see she was nervous. Part of her wanted to get up and explain to Coach Seville how Vanessa and the other girls ganged up on Angel, but she didn't want to snitch.

As Angel stood up, someone behind Jamee giggled. Other girls whispered. Coach Seville shot another dark look into the bleachers, and the noise stopped.

"Why don't you try it again?" she said to Angel gently. It was as if the coach

73

wanted her to do well.

Again Angel nodded. But when she raised her arms, Jamee noticed two dark circles of sweat in the armpits of her T-shirt, like two targets for Vanessa and her friends. Almost instantly, Jamee heard them giggling, only this time she could tell the girls were doing their best to keep it quiet so Coach Seville wouldn't call them out. Angel must have noticed, too, because her eyes flicked down to her shirt, and she looked as if she wanted to escape to the bleachers. She rushed into another cartwheel that was almost as bad as the first one.

Coach Seville scribbled in her clipboard. "Thank you, Angel," she said.

"I g-guess I'm not really that good at tumbling, Coach Seville," she confessed timidly.

"You're not the only one," Coach Seville replied, reviewing the next name on her list.

Tell them the truth, Jamee wanted to say. *Tell them what those girls did. Tell them you're nervous.*

Instead, Angel walked back to the bleachers.

"She's done," Vanessa whispered with an I-told-you-so grin. "Just like I said."

But just before Angel sat down, she stopped and shook her head as if she was talking to herself. Then she turned around and headed back to the mats in front of the bleachers. Her face looked different somehow. Her jaw looked firm, and there was a determined look in her eyes. *Did she hear Vanessa?* Jamee wondered.

"Can I try one more time?" she asked. This time her eyes weren't focused on the floor. She looked right at Coach Seville.

"Sure," the coach replied.

Angel paused, took a couple of short running steps and then did a perfect aerial, a kind of mid-air cartwheel where hands never touch the ground. Jamee's mouth dropped open. She had never been able to do one, but Angel stuck hers perfectly.

"Woo hoo!" cheered Crystal. "That's what I'm talking about." Several other Varsity cheerleaders clapped their hands. In the bleachers, most of the girls' mouths hung open in surprise.

Even Coach Seville looked stunned. "Can you do that again?" she asked.

Angel paused again as if she was focusing, and then she did another perfect aerial.

"Let me get this straight. You can't do a regular cartwheel, but you can do one with no hands?"

Angel nodded. "I was nervous," she explained, glancing once toward Vanessa and her friends but saying nothing.

Coach Seville laughed. "Well, you certainly are full of surprises," she replied with a smile. "Now go on and take a seat. Next!"

Another girl ran to the mats as Angel hurried back to the bleachers and sat down by herself on the last row. Jamee glanced up at Vanessa. Her arms were folded across her chest and her eyebrows were drawn tight together as if she was concentrating.

When the last girl had finished, Coach Seville thanked everyone. "Tomorrow will be your last day to practice all your skills before the audition," she announced. "Crystal, Michelle, and Julesa will be available to help with the chant or the routine or your jumps—anything you think you need to work on. Nice work today, ladies. It's too bad I can't choose you all!" She then clapped her hands and dismissed everyone.

In the locker room, Jamee looked for Angel but didn't see her.

"She probably isn't in any hurry to change in front of those girls again," Amberlynn said softly, nodding toward Vanessa and Tasha. "I'm not going to change, either," she added as she grabbed her clothes and books from her locker. "My mom has to be at work at four, so I have to watch my little brothers again. Wanna come over and help?"

Jamee shook her head. "I can't. I told Dez I'd meet him at the park. Then I gotta study for this math test in Mrs. Guessner's class. That woman won't get off my back." She quickly told Amberlynn about the bad grade and the retake.

Amberlynn frowned. "But how are you gonna do that, Jamee? The tryouts are Thursday after school at the same time!"

Jamee shrugged. "I'll think of something, I guess," she muttered, though she still wasn't sure what.

Jamee spotted Desmond sitting on a bench on the edge of the park when she arrived. He smiled and got up as soon as he saw her.

"Hey, Dez," Jamee said as he opened

his arms for a hug.

"Hey," he murmured, pulling her close to him.

Jamee relaxed. They were alone, and it was nice to be hugged. She could feel his heart beating beneath her ear as his arms circled tighter, pressing her closer. For a moment, Jamee forgot about Mrs. Guessner, about cheerleading, about Darcy and the new computer, about Vanessa and what she had said about her reputation.

But then his hands slid lower, toward her backside.

Jamee pushed away a bit. "Dez—" she began, but he silenced her with a sudden hungry kiss. His hands sank down her back again.

Jamee twisted away from him.

"Cut it out!" she cried.

"What?" Dez looked puzzled. "What did I do?"

"You're all over me!" Jamee turned away.

"I just gave you a kiss." Desmond put on his smooth voice. "I'm just trying to make you feel good, baby."

"Oh, cut it out," Jamee muttered.

Dez shook his head. "I just don't understand you, girl," he said in his normal voice. "We been together all summer. You never stopped me kissing you before. And from what I heard you never stopped Bobby Wallace neither, and you two were only together for like, what? A month? What, you like him more than you like me?" he said, shrugging his shoulders.

"What?" Jamee cried, stunned at what she was hearing. "You think I went all the way with Bobby Wallace? Is that what you're sayin'?"

Dez looked unsure, as if he realized that he had said more than he meant to. "Well . . . no, you know   some people were talkin' and—"

"What people?" Jamee demanded. "You tell me who's been sayin' that!"

Dez wouldn't look her in the eye. "Just some people. Don't matter who. The point is—"

"The point is what you heard ain't true! I can't believe you'd think somethin' like that 'bout me, Desmond. And no, I didn't like Bobby more than you, but maybe I *should* have. I can't believe this," Jamee yelled, walking away from him.

"*Jamee*—"

"I don't want to talk to you right

now," she fumed without turning around.

"C'mon, J! I didn't mean it like that," he called. Then a second later, "You still meetin' me for pizza after school tomorrow?"

Jamee didn't answer. Was this what Vanessa meant when she said Jamee had "quite the reputation?" Who else thought that? Did the whole school believe this story about Jamee and Bobby? And who had started the story in the first place? The questions flooded Jamee's mind for the rest of the evening.

"You're awful quiet, Jamee," her father said when he came home for a quick meal between jobs. "Is everything okay?"

"Fine," Jamee tried to smile. She couldn't bring herself to tell Dad what she had learned. "Just tired from cheerleading."

He nodded. "You makin' sure your grades are where they should be?" he asked. "I don't want to be sitting in that counselor's office again anytime soon, you hear?"

"Don't worry," Jamee said, trying to hide the guilt she felt twisting in her gut.

She made a silent promise to study right after dinner.

But when the time came, Jamee's mind kept wandering. She thought about Dez and Bobby Wallace, about Angel and Vanessa, and she couldn't help wondering just what Dez and Vanessa really heard about her. She wanted to ask Darcy what she knew but was pretty sure that would only make things worse. In the end, Jamee drifted off to sleep without doing any homework at all.

At Bluford the next day, Jamee was relieved that Mrs. Guessner didn't say anything to her in algebra class—though she was strangely cold whenever she looked in Jamee's direction. As soon as the bell rang, Jamee gathered her books and darted out the door.

Dez appeared by her side only seconds later.

"Jamee," he said falling into step beside her. "About yesterday—"

"I don't want to talk about it," Jamee mumbled. Almost by instinct, she looked around to see if anyone was watching them.

"I just wanted to say I'm sorry. I was

wrong, okay? I—" he lowered his voice. "I never shoulda believed that stuff 'bout you and Bobby. I just thought, you know, Bobby being the kind of guy he was that, well . . . you two probably had, you know . . . " he finished awkwardly.

Jamee was about to tell him off for what he had said and what he had been thinking, but then she spotted Tasha talking with a group of girls nearby.

"Look, I can't talk to you about this now. Okay?"

"You still gonna meet me at Niko's?" He flashed her his player smile.

Jamee thought about it. She could see Tasha watching them out of the corner of her eye. If she and Dez argued now, Tasha would know. Jamee didn't want Tasha in her business.

"Okay," Jamee said, but her heart wasn't in it. Something had changed. She was seeing Dez in a whole new way.

Dez leaned over and planted a kiss on her cheek as if all was forgiven.

"See you at Niko's, then," he said, turning back up the hallway toward his class.

Nearby Tasha watched, flashing a fake smile as if the incident in the locker room never happened.

"Hey Jamee!" Crystal said when Jamee joined the girls in the gym for the final practice before auditions. "You've been looking great out there. I think you've got a good shot to make the team tomorrow. I'm about to lead a group who want to go over the step routine." She nodded toward a cluster of girls waiting on the edge of the gym. "Wanna join in?"

Jamee looked around. Amberlynn wasn't there yet, but Angel was standing with the small group, looking around as if she expected someone to pounce on her at any minute. In another corner, Julesa had a group of girls working on some of the jumps. Coach Seville had a smaller group at the far edge of the gym working on some tumbling moves. Vanessa and her friends were with this group. While Jamee watched, Vanessa attempted an aerial and landed on her behind.

"Sure." Jamee grinned and took a spot beside Angel.

"Hi, Jamee." Angel's smile lit up her face.

"You know what, Angel?" Jamee said looking back at her. "You need to do more of that."

"What?"

"Smile like that," Jamee said. "I'm serious."

"She's right," Crystal said. "And be sure you do it tomorrow during your audition. Good cheerleaders always do their routines with a big smile on their face. Seriously, think about the girls here who you think are good. They're always smilin'."

Angel nodded thoughtfully. "Okay," she said. "Thanks."

Just then Amberlynn came jogging up to Crystal's group.

"Sorry," she panted. "I had to talk to my Spanish teacher. Test next week."

Jamee thought of her algebra class. A wave of dread spread over her, and she rubbed her forehead. Just then, Crystal clapped her hands to get their attention.

"C'mon. Let's go, everyone!" she hollered.

The small group of girls took their places, and Jamee pushed Mrs. Guessner from her mind again. It was the most fun she had in weeks. With Vanessa and her friends on the other side of the gym, Jamee was able to relax. She and Amberlynn ended up working with Angel the entire time. For once, the skinny girl actually laughed and smiled and cheered her heart out. Jamee liked her.

"Excellent work, ladies!" Coach Seville bellowed across the gym. Jamee looked at the clock. Practice was over already. The time had gone so quickly, Jamee was surprised.

"Tomorrow is the big day," the coach continued. "When you get here, there will be a list on the bulletin board indicating your audition group. Crystal and Julesa will let in one group at a time. Come in full of spirit. I want to see your jumps, your flips—all the energy you can give me. Then you'll do your cheer routine and you're done. Results will be on the board Friday morning. Got it?"

"Yes, Coach!" everyone shouted. Jamee glanced at Angel and smiled.

"All right, girls. Get a good night's sleep. Good luck to you all!"

"Thanks, you two," Angel said, looking at Jamee and Amberlynn. "I had fun." She grabbed her backpack from under the bleachers and slipped it over her shoulders.

"You'll be here tomorrow, right?" Amberlynn asked.

"You bet," Angel grinned, then waved at them and walked away.

"I gotta watch my brothers again, but if you wanna come over, we could practice some more while we keep an eye on them," Amberlynn suggested.

Jamee shook her head. "I promised Dez I'd meet him after this."

Amberlynn smiled. "I don't blame you. I'd choose Dez over my brothers, too. See you tomorrow?"

"Yeah, see you."

But instead of leaving, Jamee sat back down on the locker room bench. She knew Dez was waiting, but for the first time, she didn't feel like seeing him. She had always had a boyfriend—at least since the start of middle school— but now she wondered if that was a mistake. She changed out of her sweaty T-shirt and shorts as slowly as possible. The locker room emptied as the other girls grabbed their belongings and left.

Jamee ignored them all, even Vanessa's mean laugh and Tasha's odd, guilty stare.

Chapter 6

"Girl, it's about time," Dez complained as Jamee walked into Niko's. "Where you been?"

Something about his question made her so angry that she couldn't answer. It didn't help that Darcy, Hakeem, Cooper, and Tarah were there too, listening to every word.

"And don't say, 'at tryouts'," he added, resting his arms on her shoulders as if she was his property. "They were at the tryouts, too, and they've been sitting there for about five minutes."

Tasha, Vanessa, Renita, and Kym were sitting in the corner. Vanessa held Tasha's pink phone between her long nails. The girls were hunched close like animals at a feeding. They cackled loudly several times as they looked at

87

something on the tiny screen.

"Great," Jamee muttered, ignoring Dez's question. "This is just great."

"What's the matter, girl?" Tarah asked. She slid the pizza they had ordered toward her.

"Nothing," Jamee sighed, not wanting to explain it. "I'm just tired."

"I'd be tired, too, if I was you," Cooper joked. "Listenin' to his big mouth all day is enough to wear anyone out," he said, looking at Dez.

"Man, why you gotta be like that, Coop?" Dez protested.

"'Cause you always bugging her, that's why! You ever see what the coach has them girls doin'? I used to think cheerleading was all pom-poms and stuff. But one day I passed by the gym after school, and the coach had all the girls doing backflips and step dances. That's no joke. I could never do that."

"So what were you doin' watchin' them cheerleaders in the first place?" Tarah cut in, raising an eyebrow at her boyfriend.

"Uh oh," Hakeem said with a smile. "You walked right into that, Coop."

"Aw c'mon, T! It wasn't like that," Cooper insisted.

"Mmm hmm," Tarah said, a teasing glint in her eye. Dez ignored them both.

"But that still don't answer my question. Why are you so late?" he asked.

"Coach Seville wanted to talk to me, okay," Jamee lied. She didn't want to admit that she had sat alone in the locker room wishing she didn't have to go to Niko's or that she was still bothered by what Dez had said the other day. Even though he apologized, she still thought about her reputation and how he had expected her to kiss him whenever he wanted—or maybe go further. Maybe that was why he wanted to go out with her in the first place. The thought made her stomach churn.

"Why didn't you say so?" Dez answered, squeezing her a bit tighter. His sweaty skin clung to the back of her neck. She felt trapped, almost claustrophobic. Having Vanessa and the other girls so close only made it worse. She wanted to shrug him off and walk out, but she couldn't think of a way to do it without making a scene.

"I hope your coach wasn't talking to you about your grades," Darcy chimed in. "They treat the cheerleaders just like athletes. You'll have to keep your grades up to—"

"That's because we *are* athletes. And no, it wasn't about my grades, okay?" Jamee snapped. "It was something else." Her eyes strayed toward Vanessa and her friends. She wondered what they were staring at on the tiny screen.

"No need to get upset," Darcy muttered. "I'm just trying to help—"

"Well, you can help by staying out of my business," Jamee snapped, the frustration of the past few days boiling over inside her. "Did you ever think I might get sick of hearing about what a great student you are compared to me? 'Are you Darcy's sister?' 'I'd expect better from Darcy's sister.' Blah, blah, blah."

Darcy blinked at her in surprise. "I'm sorry, Jamee. I just meant—"

"Yeah, I know what you meant." Jamee rolled her eyes. "But maybe if I make cheerleader, you'll get some of what I've been dealing with. Maybe someone will ask you if you're Jamee Wills's sister instead of the other way around. In the meantime, just leave me alone."

Darcy recoiled as if she had just been slapped. Tarah grunted, while Cooper grabbed another slice of pizza in silence. For a long time no one spoke, as if they were too scared to get involved in a fight between sisters. Jamee wished she had skipped Niko's and gone straight home.

"Hey, Jamee," Dez said when the silence got thick enough to taste. "Your girls over there are checking you out."

Jamee turned toward the corner booth. She caught Tasha's eye for a split second just as Vanessa whispered something to her. Tasha giggled, but Jamee could tell it was forced. Tasha almost seemed uncomfortable—the way she had looked the day Vanessa borrowed her phone.

What are they up to? Jamee wondered.

Just then Renita leaned close and said something into Vanessa's ear. All of the girls stopped talking and turned their heads back toward the door. Jamee followed their stares.

Angel McAllister walked into the restaurant still wearing the shorts and T-shirt she had on at practice. A thin little girl with the same round face and dark coffee bean eyes held her hand.

Is that Angel's little sister? Jamee wondered. The way she looked up at Angel as they approached the counter made her think so.

91

"Hey, ain't that the skinny girl Vanessa was doggin' the other day?" Dez asked.

"Her name is Angel," Jamee snapped. As she watched, Vanessa slid from her booth and started toward Angel and her sister. Jamee had a bad feeling. Without a word, she rose from her chair and moved toward the counter. Dez and the others looked surprised as she passed, but Jamee couldn't explain, not now.

"What's up, Angel?" Jamee said, darting in front of Vanessa. She could tell from Vanessa's expression that she had gotten in her way and stopped her from doing something rude. "I didn't know you came to Niko's."

"I don't," Angel said, nervously eyeing Vanessa. "This is my first time here. I heard they have the best pizza around, so my mom sent us here to get one." Jamee could tell Angel was uncomfortable.

"What are you doing, Jamee?" Vanessa grumbled, her eyes narrowing.

"Nothin'. Just saying hi to my girl, that's all," Jamee replied, raising her voice so everyone at her table could hear. She figured Vanessa wouldn't start anything if she knew Darcy and Tarah were watching, too. "That okay with you?"

Vanessa glanced over at her table and gave a quick, fake smile, but her eyes were anything but happy. Angel quickly ordered her pizza. Her little sister hovered by her waist.

"So you gonna do your aerial for the audition tomorrow, Angel?" Jamee continued. She hoped the pizza would be done quickly and Angel and her sister could get away before anything bad happened. "If we all make the team, you'll have to teach us how to do it. Maybe even you, Vanessa."

"There's more to cheerleading than aerials, Jamee," Vanessa snarled.

"Yeah, but it docsn't hurt her chances, docs it?" Jamee replied. She wanted Angel to hear her. She looked so nervous, so scared whenever Vanessa was around. And yet, Angel had something special. Jamee wanted her to remember it the night before auditions. She knew Vanessa would try to rip it away.

"Whatever," Vanessa huffed. "It's not enough, especially not for her."

"Here you go," interrupted the guy working the counter. He slid a box toward Angel. "That's ten dollars."

Angel let go of the little girl's hand and gave him a crushed wad of bills.

Then she grabbed the pizza box. "See you, Jamee," she said quickly. "Come on, Dionne. Let's go—"

Vanessa's hand flashed out the instant Angel shifted her attention to her sister. The pizza box tipped precariously and began to spill toward the floor. But Jamee reached forward and grabbed it first.

"Whoa," she muttered as the box leveled out in Angel's hands again. "That was close."

Angel stared at Vanessa for what felt like forever. Jamee could feel the battle going on between them.

"Angel . . . let's go," Dionne whispered. "I'm hungry."

The little girl's voice broke Angel's stare. She grabbed the pizza with both hands this time and turned toward the door.

"I'm not going to quit, Vanessa," she said softly. "Coach Seville might not pick me, but I'm not going to quit. I don't care what you do." She nodded at Jamee. "Thanks, Jamee. I wouldn't have had enough money to buy another one."

"No problem."

"I'll teach you the aerial any time you want."

Jamee grinned. "I'd like that."

Angel's little sister lifted her fingers in a wave and gave Jamee a smile as they left. Jamee would have returned to her table, but Vanessa stepped in her way.

"You just made a big mistake, Jamee," she hissed. "I gave you a chance, but it's over now." There was a smudge of mascara under her right eye that made her look like someone had punched her. The smudge and the angry sneer on her face made her suddenly look very, very ugly.

"Is everything okay?" Dez had gotten up from the table. Darcy, Hakeem, Tarah, and Cooper walked up behind him.

"Everything's fine." Vanessa's voice dripped with honey, but her eyes glinted with anger.

"We've got to get home, Jamee," Darcy said.

"Yes, you get home, Jamee," Vanessa said in a sugary tone as fake as cotton candy. "I'll see you tomorrow."

Jamee could hear the threat in her voice even if no one else could. She walked out of Niko's uneasily, wondering what Vanessa was up to.

"Why did you do that to me, Jamee?" Darcy asked as soon as they got outside and everyone split up. Her voice was almost shaking with anger. "Why did you embarrass me like that in front of my friends?"

"You do it to me all the time!"

"All I said was—"

"That I was stupid! That I have bad grades and I'm gonna get kicked off the cheering squad right after I make it—"

"That's not what I said!" Darcy yelled so loudly that people on the street turned and stared.

"But that's what you meant. It's what you always mean when you talk to me, Darcy. Like you think I'm too dumb to do anything so you gotta nag me all the time. Admit it."

"Forget it," Darcy muttered. "There's no use talking to you sometimes." She turned and walked briskly down the street, her arms wrapped tightly around her books.

Jamee stood on the corner trembling with anger as her sister disappeared down the block.

Everything suddenly seemed so complicated: her relationship with Darcy, her feelings about Dez, her performance in school, the cheerleading tryouts. It seemed as if everybody was pressuring her to be someone else.

Her family and teachers wanted her to be Darcy. Vanessa wanted her to be like Tasha and pick on Angel for no reason. Dez wanted her to be the girl with the bad reputation.

But Jamee wanted none of this. And yet the more she tried to be herself, the more trouble she got into. Confused and uncertain, Jamee reluctantly followed Darcy home.

"In here!" Dad called when Jamee finally reached the house. His voice had an urgent sound to it.

Jamee sighed. She figured that Darcy told him they had gotten into an argument at Niko's. Now she would have to explain to Dad what happened.

Thanks a lot, Darcy, she thought. *As if making my life miserable at school isn't enough.*

She trudged toward the sound of her father's voice, expecting to find him in her parents' room. But instead, the door to Grandma's room stood wide open. A hint of Grandma's lilac perfume still hung in the air. It almost seemed as if Grandma herself were inside ready to greet her with her smile.

Instead Dad was sitting on the floor

wearing an old T-shirt. Sweat darkened his shirt beneath his arms and along his back. Mom sat next to him in Grandma's old rocking chair wiping her eyes with a wad of tissues. Darcy stood in front of them. They were staring at an open cardboard box. No one looked up when Jamee walked in.

"What's going on?" she asked.

"Well, your father took some time off to go to the doctor with me today, and we figured it's time." Her mother shrugged her shoulders a bit. "Grandma's been gone over three months and we got to start making room for this baby, so . . ."

Jamee looked around. Until today, the room had been left exactly as it had been when Grandma was alive, but now Jamee noticed that her curtains were gone, and the windows looked stark and bare. Two of the dresser drawers were open and clothes were scattered on her bed. When Jamee glanced at the closet, she could see that all of Grandma's shoes were gone.

Jamee swallowed down a lump in her throat. Grandma had died in this room. Jamee shook remembering the morning they found her silent and still in her bed. After her stroke and a long, slow decline, she had passed peacefully in her sleep, taking her voice, her wisdom, and her comforting presence with her. It didn't seem right to throw all her things in a box as if she had never been there. Jamee blinked hard to keep tears from rolling down her face.

"I know," Mom said, gently touching her shoulder. "You can really feel her spirit in this room. But she'd be the first one to tell us to move on. I can hear her in my head right now. She's saying, 'Mattie, you get that room ready for my grandchild, y'hear. A baby needs that space more than I do!'"

Mom sounded just like Grandma. Jamee wanted to both laugh and cry. Even though what Mom said made sense, Jamee didn't want to let go of Grandma's room. Somehow it made it seem as if she was still nearby, ready to listen when no one else would. Jamee wished she could talk to her right now.

"Are you getting rid of everything?" she asked, trying to hide her thoughts.

Mom shook her head. "No. We're keeping the things that meant the most to her. But she wouldn't want us holding onto her clothes forever, especially when someone else could wear them. You understand, right?"

Jamee nodded, but understanding didn't make it any easier. Her throat felt as if she had swallowed a basketball. She hated watching Grandma's room being torn apart, no matter what the reason.

"Darcy's packing up her dresser. Maybe you can do the closet. Here." Dad held out a box of plastic bags to her. Mom watched her from the rocking chair.

"If you see something important that you want to keep, I want you to take it. Grandma would want you to, okay?"

Jamee could feel her parents watching her. She knew they meant well, but it still didn't seem right. Yet what could she do?

Without a word, Jamee grabbed the plastic bags and began removing Grandma's blouses and skirts from the closet. On one hanger, she found an old gray sweater Grandma used to wear. Stuck on the front was a button Jamee had made for her on Mother's Day in Ms. Kopec's first-grade class. "World's Greatest Grandma," it read in awkward pink letters around a picture Jamee drew of herself in crayon.

At the time, Jamee thought her picture was perfect. Now she realized it looked silly and sloppy. Yet Grandma wore it as if it were a priceless treasure. Jamee wondered if she was just being nice or if she really did like it.

"Look at this!" Darcy said, breaking her thoughts. She held a big black hat with a pink flower pinned on the side.

"Her Sunday hat," Mom said. "She must have worn that hat to church a thousand times before she got too sick to go." Her voice trailed off.

"Mattie," Dad went over and patted her shoulder. "You okay? You want to stop?"

"I'm okay, Carl. I just can't help thinking about how happy she would be to have a baby to hold again. She'd be smilin' ear to ear."

"Yes, she would," Dad agreed.

Jamee winced. Of course Grandma would love the baby, but why did they act as if everything would be better once the baby arrived? A baby wouldn't fix anything.

Grandma's still gone, and my life's still a mess. Jamee almost said the words out loud as she filled another bag with Grandma's clothes.

Next to her, Mom leaned forward in Grandma's rocker and stood up slowly, resting her hands on her belly. "Well, I gotta work tonight, so I'd better get changed—"

Just then, the phone rang. Darcy moved toward the door, but Mom stopped her.

"I'm up. I'll get it," she said and stepped into the hallway, swaying slightly as she walked.

"So, Darcy, how's school?" asked Dad.

"Good," Darcy answered. She then went on about what she found on the computer and how she was going to take some test called the PSAT in a few weeks.

Jamee ignored her, carefully removing the button she had made from Grandma's sweater. She had just slipped it in her pocket when she heard the phone slam down in the other room.

"Jamee Wills!" Her mother hollered from down the hallway. "Get your butt out here right now!"

"What is it, Mattie?" Dad asked.

Darcy turned and flashed Jamee the what-did-you-do-now look. Jamee almost told her off as she rushed to Mom. Dad followed right behind her.

Mom stood at the kitchen counter

with a look of fury on her face.

"What, Mom?" Jamee asked, bewildered. "What'd I do?"

"It's what you *didn't* do, according to Mrs. Guessner, your algebra teacher. That was her on the phone." She looked over Jamee's head to her father. Jamee felt her stomach sinking as her mother scowled at her.

"Apparently Jamee failed a test and was supposed to bring it home for us to sign. You seen a math test?"

Dad shook his head. "That true, Jamee?"

"Yes, but—"

"That's only part of it, Carl. Mrs. Guessner says Jamee told her we signed it."

"What?" Dad crossed his arms on his chest and shook his head.

"And she was supposed to meet her after school for extra help, but she skipped it *twice* for cheerleading practice!" Her mother fumed, the creases in her forehead deep and angry. "Jamee, if I've told you once, I've told you a thousand times, there ain't gonna be no cheerleading if you can't keep your grades up!"

"I know," Jamee tried to explain. "But Mom, it's just one stupid test and

I'm gonna retake it tomorrow—"

"Did you study? Did you go get some extra help?"

Jamee hung her head.

"No, of course not. You're too busy with cheerleaders and sneakin' around with that boy Desmond Hodden."

"I didn't sneak—"

"Mattie, remember what the doctor said, not to get upset," Dad urged, putting his hand on Mom's shoulder.

"It's too late for that, Carl!" Mom snapped, shrugging away from him and turning back to Jamee.

"You're not gonna amount to anything in this world if you keep this up. Y'hear me? The only reason you even made it through eighth grade is 'cause your teachers cut you some slack with all the problems we went through last year." Her mother flashed Dad a knowing look and shook her head as if she were disgusted.

"And after all that and our meeting this summer, you still failed your first test! And you *lied to us* about it?" Mom's voice boomed with anger.

"Mattie—"

"And for what?" she continued, glaring at Jamee. "Stupid cheerleading! I can't believe this."

Jamee knew she had been wrong to lie. Deep inside, she also knew she would never achieve as much as Darcy. But one word Mom said set off a spark in her head. *Stupid.* She couldn't hold her anger in any more.

"Cheerleading's *not* stupid!" she yelled back at her mother. "Algebra's stupid!"

"Oh, so now you got all the answers too, huh?" Mom said, stepping forward and glaring down into Jamee's face. "Let me tell you something. You better turn this around and start being more like Darcy when it comes to school, or we're gonna have some serious problems around here."

Jamee trembled in rage at Mom's words. There it was again. *Be like Darcy.* She wanted to grab her mother's shoulders and shake her.

"I'm *not* Darcy, Mom!" she shouted. "Maybe if you weren't so caught up in Darcy's testing, and Aunt Charlotte's computer, and your *stupid* plans for the baby's room, you'd see that—"

Whap!

Mom's open palm struck Jamee on the side of her face, filling her cheek with pain. Dad darted in between them

105

and gently nudged Mom back.

"Mattie, please!"

"You watch your mouth, Jamee Wills!" her mother hissed, a fiery mix of shock and fury in her eyes. "I can't even stand to look at you right now. Go to your room!"

Jamee stood still. Even though she knew she should move, her feet felt nailed to the floor.

"And tomorrow, you better pass that test, you hear me? If you don't, cheer-leading's over, and you're gonna be grounded in this house until you get your head on straight and learn to speak to me with some respect! Y'hear me?! Now go!"

Jamee didn't move. Her cheek throbbed where her mother's fingers had struck her. Tears pooled in her eyes, but she wouldn't let them fall, not with everyone staring at her, not with Darcy's mouth hanging open in disbelief.

"You can send me to my room all you want, but you can't make me care about that test," Jamee said, her chest heaving. "I'm not like *her*, okay?" Jamee jerked her head toward Darcy. "I never have been. I'm sorry if that's not good enough for any of you."

Her mother turned and rubbed her forehead as if she had a terrible headache.

"Jamee, please. Just go," Dad said in a low voice, rushing to Mom's side. "It's not good for the baby or your mother to be upset."

But what about me?! Jamee thought as she stood at the edge of the hallway alone. She could feel the tears swirling behind her eyes, and Darcy's constant stare pressing over her face. Unable to hide her tears any longer, Jamee hurried to her room and slammed the door.

Chapter 7

Knock! Knock!

Jamee opened her swollen eyes at the sound and sat up in her bed. She glanced at the clock. Hours had passed. She realized she had fallen asleep.

"Amberlynn's on the phone," Darcy called through the door. "She says it's important."

Jamee got up and stumbled to the door. Darcy stood in the hallway, looking as if she wanted to say something. Whatever it was, Jamee wasn't ready to hear it. She grabbed the phone and retreated to her room.

"Jamee?" Amberlynn sounded funny. "Have you seen it? Are you okay?"

"Seen what?"

"The picture."

"Huh?"

"Oh my God. You don't even know about it yet?!" Amberlynn exclaimed.

"Know about *what*?"

"Someone sent a nasty picture of you and Angel to everyone's cell phone."

"*What?!*" Jamee shook her head, trying to make sense of what Amberlynn was saying. "What do you mean, *nasty*?"

"Well, I don't have a cell phone, so I haven't seen it yet, but Alisha did," Amberlynn spoke quickly as if she couldn't force the words out fast enough. "She said Angel looks half-naked in it, and your arm is around her. She said it kinda looks like you're *together* or something."

"*Together?*" Jamee cried, the room seemed to spin.

"Like in *that* way."

"I understand what you mean, Amberlynn!" Jamee snapped. "But that ain't right—"

"I know, I know, Jamee," Amberlynn said earnestly. "That's why I called you. I'm just telling you what Alisha told me. She was looking at it just now."

"I don't believe this," Jamee huffed. There had to be some kind of mistake. She would never be involved with anything like what Alisha described.

Besides, she hadn't even taken any pictures with Angel. "She's wrong or she's lying. There's no way that's true."

"That's what I said, but she said I should see it. Can you meet me over there?"

Jamee rubbed her face. It was nearly 8:00, and on school nights she was supposed to be in by 7:00. But now both of her parents were at work, and only Darcy was in the house. What could she do? Besides, Jamee knew she was in a ton of trouble already. How could it get any worse, even if Darcy told on her?

"I'm on my way," she said.

Darcy stood in the hallway, stern-faced, with her arms crossed on her chest. Maybe she had been listening. Jamee couldn't tell.

"Where are you going?" Darcy demanded as Jamee rushed toward the front door.

"Out," she answered, without stopping.

"Mom and Dad said—"

"I don't care what they said," Jamee grumbled. "This is important."

Darcy crossed her arms and stood between Jamee and the door. "I can't let you do this, Jamee. When Mom and Dad find out—"

"They're not going to find out unless you tell them, Darcy."

"Don't do this, Jamee. Whatever it is, it's not that important. After everything that happened tonight, you need to stay home and study. I can help you. You need to pass that test."

"And you need to get outta my face, Darcy," Jamee warned. Her hands trembled, and she glared into her sister's eyes. She would knock her aside if she had to. Though Darcy was older, Jamee knew she could overpower her sister, especially with the way she felt right now. She was sure Darcy knew it, too.

"You can't run away again, Jamee! I won't let you. You can't do that to Mom, not with the baby."

"I'm not running away! I'm going to Alisha's," she grumbled. "Now move."

Darcy paused and shook her head as if she knew she couldn't stop her. Then she stepped aside.

"Whatever you do, I'm not gonna cover for you."

"Then don't," Jamee said angrily.

She shouldered past Darcy and stepped out alone into the cool, dark evening.

Jamee couldn't believe what she saw.

On the tiny screen of Alisha's phone was a picture just like Amberlynn had described. Angel wore a white sports bra and slumped forward looking upset, almost teary. Without a shirt on, her torso was long and wiry, and her chest was pointy and small. Jamee sat close to her, an almost tender look on her face. Her arm rested gently on Angel's bare shoulders. The picture even contained a short caption.

"Look who's in love," it said.

Jamee almost smashed Alisha's phone against the wall. She knew the picture was taken the day Vanessa and her friends stole Angel's shirt. She could even see the hazy image of a locker behind Angel's head.

"Vanessa did this! I know it," Jamee fumed, barely able to contain her anger. "I can't believe her."

"Yeah, but she probably didn't take the picture herself. She's smarter than that," Amberlynn said. "I bet she got one of her friends to do it for her."

Jamee studied the image again. The person who took it had to be standing at the corner of the row of lockers. And then it clicked.

Tasha.

It all made sense. No wonder Tasha had been looking so guilty lately. No wonder she'd been standing there fiddling with her cell phone the day it happened. No wonder Vanessa and her friends were hunched over her cell phone at Niko's.

Jamee told Amberlynn and Alisha everything that happened at the pizzeria. "Now I know why they were laughing," she added, her hands flexing with anger.

"Yeah, they were probably pressing *Send* on your picture right then," Amberlynn said.

"I still can't believe she sent it to the whole school like that. That girl is messed up!" Alisha said.

Jamee couldn't believe it either. The more she thought about it, the more she wanted to rip out Vanessa's hair extensions and smack Tasha in the face with them.

"I guess she meant it when she threatened you," Amberlynn added.

"Yeah, well I'm gonna take that girl down. There ain't no way she's gonna get away with this."

"You can't just fight her, Jamee," Amberlynn frowned. "If you do that,

113

they'll suspend you from school and throw you off the squad. That's exactly what Vanessa wants to happen."

"Look, if they did this to keep Angel off the cheerleading squad, all you gotta do is tell Coach Seville. She'll kick 'em off the squad in two seconds. And that way you'll still have a chance to be on the team," Alisha suggested.

Jamee shook her head. She hadn't told on anyone in years, not even if she knew some of the kids who sold drugs after school, stole from cars on Union Street, or busted the swings in the nearby park. Ratting people out didn't seem right. But maybe now was different.

"I hate to say it, but Alisha's right," Amberlynn agreed. "Besides, you don't wanna fight all them girls. I know you're crazy sometimes, but some of them look kinda fierce."

"I don't care who they are," Jamee snapped. "They're gonna have the whole school talking about me!" She could almost hear the laughter as people checked out their messages and saw the picture. She knew others would look at it and think it was real, more proof of her wild reputation. Dez might be one of them. The thought made her stomach twist.

What if it gets online on SpaceBook or MyFace? Jamee wondered and then cursed out loud.

"Calm down, Jamee. It's no big deal. Just tell Coach Seville tomorrow. She'll boot Vanessa and Tasha out before auditions even start. The whole thing'll be over just like that." Alisha snapped her fingers to make her point.

"You don't get it, Alisha! How would you feel if strangers were staring at *you?!*"

Alisha shut her mouth, and for a moment the three girls were silent.

"Do you think Angel has seen these pictures?" Amberlynn asked finally. "It might be worse for her. No one even knows her."

Jamee shook her head. She hadn't even thought about Angel. As shy and alone as she was at Bluford, the picture would be devastating. "I don't know."

Alisha frowned. "Well, if Vanessa wants her to drop out of the tryouts, she'd probably make *sure* she saw it. That's what I would do if I were them."

"Yeah, but Angel doesn't have a cell phone. I bet she doesn't even know about this," Amberlynn said.

"No matter what, she's gonna find out tomorrow," said Alisha soberly.

115

Jamee stared at the tiny image again. Each time she looked at it, she felt angrier. Part of her wanted to fight Vanessa and Tasha first thing tomorrow and tell the entire school what they had done. Another part was so embarrassed she didn't want to set foot in Bluford again.

But then she thought about Angel. She was the one who was half-naked. She was the one everyone would see. She was the one who had no friends at Bluford. Someone had to look out for her.

"So whatcha gonna do?" Amberlynn asked.

Jamee tossed Alisha's phone aside and stood up, her forehead pounding. There was so much pressing down on her—Mrs. Guessner and the stupid test, the fight with Mom and Dad, the nonsense with Dez, the stress of cheerleading auditions. And now this. Jamee felt as if her skull was about to explode.

"I don't know."

They talked for a few more minutes before Jamee hurried home with her head heavy and aching. Darcy was still sitting in the living room when Jamee came back in.

"I need to talk to you," she said as

soon as Jamee closed the front door. "I just got off the phone with Tarah. She told me there's some picture of you going around school. Jamee if you're in some kind of trouble—"

"It's *my* business, Darcy," Jamee muttered.

"Jamee," Darcy frowned. "You're my sister. I know you think we're in some kinda . . . competition, but that's not true. I just want to help—"

"I don't need your help," Jamee barked. "I can handle this on my own."

She went straight to her room and closed the door.

"Yo, Jamee!" Dez called, an edge to his voice. He was waiting outside her house Thursday morning.

"What are you doin' here?" she asked sharply. She felt as if she had barely slept. Her head was hurting already, and the day hadn't even started.

"You know why I'm here. Don't act stupid!" he snorted.

"Don't start with me, Dez. I'm not in the mood."

"I knew you'd been acting funny. Like you don't like me no more. But another *girl?* Why you gonna do me like that?"

"Listen, Dez. It ain't what it looks like—"

"Right," he muttered. "I saw how you jumped up as soon as she walked into Niko's yesterday. You left me sittin' there like some kind of fool!" He shook his head. "If you were *that* way, you should have never started going out with me. Or you could have broken up with me instead of humiliating me like this—"

"Humiliating *you!*" Jamee scoffed. "Is that all you can think about? First you accuse me of doing it with Bobby Wallace, and now you actually think I was with Angel McAllister! Forget you, Desmond. You think I shoulda' broke up with you earlier? Well I'm doin' it now. I'm done with you. Goodbye. Don't talk to me no more—"

"You're done with *me?*" Desmond's eyes flared as she passed him. "I'm not the one with her hands all over another *girl*—"

She turned back, barely able to stop herself from slapping him.

"Desmond, I can't believe I *ever* went out with you!" Jamee screamed, stopping just inches from his face. "If I was into girls, I'da told you before I ever kissed you. But you know what? It don't matter. All you wanted was some girl with a

118

reputation so you could get with her any-time you feel like it. Well, that ain't me neither, no matter what you heard!"

Jamee turned and stormed away as quickly as she could. She was relieved that Desmond didn't try to keep up with her. By the time she reached the school, he was more than a block behind.

"Yo, Jamee! Where's your girlfriend, huh?" two guys she didn't know hollered as she walked up the cement steps to school. "When you gonna come back to our side?"

As she neared her locker, a group of sophomore girls eyed her as if she had a disease. Jamee could tell they were talk-ing about her. She wondered if Angel was going through the same thing. Was she still as determined to succeed as she had been yesterday? Or had the picture changed her mind? Maybe Angel had gone straight to Coach Seville this morn-ing. What if she quit the team?

"Can you believe them two were together?" one of the girls mumbled.

"Yeah, and last year she dated that drug dealer."

"And then she got busted for shop-lifting."

"No wonder she ran away. That girl is

119

a mess."

Jamee cringed. The words set fire to her insides. She was about to yell back at them that it was none of their business, that the rumors were wrong, but the girls turned and walked up an unfamiliar corridor. Rather than follow them, she darted to Mrs. Guessner's class, keeping her head down to avoid the stares.

But the snickers and comments followed her. Jamee couldn't believe how quickly Bluford had turned on her. It was as if the entire high school was a beast thirsty for gossip and hungry for someone to humiliate. Had it always been this way? She had never noticed it before, maybe because she always had an older sister to shield her. But now, thanks to Vanessa and her friends, Jamee realized she had become a target.

As she turned the corner to Mrs. Guessner's class, Jamee stopped in her tracks. Vanessa stood before her in the center of a cluster of girls crowded against a row of lockers. Some of them laughed loudly. Jamee recognized a few faces, including Tasha, but others were new. Clutched in Vanessa's right hand was Tasha's pink cell phone. Tasha watched it intently, almost as if trying to grab it with her eyes. But Vanessa held on to it, pressing buttons quickly, her fingers like needles stabbing at the tiny keys.

"I couldn't *believe* it, either!" she was saying. "I mean, I'm not surprised about Angel, but Jamee Wills? Doesn't she have a boyfriend?"

"*Had.* Desmond Hodden just broke up with her. This morning," said one of the girls eagerly, as if she enjoyed sharing the news with Vanessa.

"I guess you don't know about some people," Kym added with a smirk.

"You all know that's not true!" Jamee yelled, unable to stop herself from walking toward them, even though she was alone. Several girls gaped in surprise. Tasha stepped back, avoiding her gaze, while Kym flashed a mean grin.

"Here we go," Kym said, dropping her backpack.

Jamee stepped up to Vanessa, staring at the taller girl's hair extensions and the cover-up she wore to make herself look pretty. All Jamee could see was ugliness in Vanessa's lying eyes. She wanted nothing more than to slap the grin from her mouth right there, though

Kym stepped right up to Vanessa's side.

"It's a lie and you know it, Vanessa," Jamee hissed.

"Girl you're trippin', and you're about to get yourself in trouble," Vanessa warned.

"I know what you did. I saw you holding that phone yesterday at Niko's. I know you got Tasha to take that picture."

"Really?" Vanessa crinkled her brow. "Did I force you to take a picture, Tasha?"

Tasha glanced at Jamee, then hung her head without saying anything. Vanessa glared at her.

"I don't know why you don't just admit it, Jamee. So what if you have a thing for Angel? Besides, the picture isn't on this phone. Tasha wouldn't keep anything like that on here. See?" Vanessa smirked as she held out the phone. The screen was blank, as if everything had been erased.

Whap! Jamee reached out and smacked the phone from her hand. It tumbled to the ground, where Tasha quickly grabbed it. Kym shoved Jamee back. Voices whooped and hollered.

"They're gonna fight!" someone shouted.

"Girl fight!" The calls echoed down the hallway. People gathered around.

"Tell them what you did," Jamee ordered, her fingers curling into fists as she glared at the two girls.

Vanessa didn't even flinch.

"I ain't done nothing to you. And if you think I did, prove it," she said with a wicked sneer on her face.

"C'mon, girl. If you're so bad, bring it!" Kym taunted.

It was too much. Jamee was about to throw a punch when a classroom door suddenly swung open.

Mrs. Guessner stepped out into the hallway. Overhead, the warning bell rang. Students had one minute to get to class.

"What's going on here?" Mrs. Guessner demanded as her eyes swept between Jamee and Vanessa, and then at the students gathering around. "The second bell is about to ring. If you know what's good for you, you'll all get to class. Now!" she said loudly.

The crowd scattered. Vanessa tossed her hair and walked away with a smirk.

"Jamee Wills, get in here right now," Mrs. Guessner ordered. Jamee shook with anger as she raced to her seat and pretended she didn't see everyone staring at her.

"That's what I'm talking about," called out Ahmad, a boy who snuck in just before the bell. He eyed Jamee as he sat down. "Girls gone wild!" A few of the other boys laughed. Mrs. Guessner raised an eyebrow.

"Ahmad," she said sternly. "Since you're eager for attention this morning, why don't you come up and solve the first problem on the blackboard?"

Ahmad groaned as he pulled himself out of his chair. Jamee pretended to watch him as he struggled to solve the equation the teacher had written, but it was all an act. She kept blinking fast to keep from crying.

As the class dragged on, Jamee couldn't stop replaying the events in the hallway. If Mrs. Guessner hadn't come out when she did, Jamee knew she would have hit Vanessa for sure. Then she would have ended up in Principal Spencer's office. Her parents would have been called. Cheerleading would be over. It would have been exactly what Vanessa wanted. She would have won.

"I'm not gonna let her beat me," she wrote in her notebook.

Writing the words seemed to calm

her anger, so Jamee wrote again.

"I'm not gonna let her beat me. I'm gonna find a way to turn this around," she wrote. *"I'm gonna turn this around and everyone's gonna see Vanessa for the* liar *she is."*

Jamee underlined the word liar so hard her pencil broke, but she didn't care. For the first time all morning, she took a deep breath. She still had no idea how she would get Vanessa to admit what she had done, but at least her head was clear enough to think.

"Don't forget, those of you retaking the test today need to be here right after school!" Mrs. Guessner called over the bell at the end of the period. "There won't be any second chances after this!"

Jamee heard her, but she had already made up her mind what she would be doing after school. She had hoped to sneak out of the class without having to face Mrs. Guessner, but the teacher stopped her before she made it past her desk.

"Jamee," she said in a low voice and then waited until the classroom emptied out. "I guess you know I spoke with your mother yesterday. I explained to her that you're in jeopardy of failing this course and that we really need to get a handle on it before it's too late. Understand?"

Jamee nodded.

"Good. So you're going to show up and take this test today?"

Jamee hesitated. She knew she could just say yes . . . and then skip the test later. But right at that moment, Jamee knew the last thing she needed was another lie.

"No, Mrs. Guessner. I'm not gonna retake the test this afternoon. I have to go to cheerleading tryouts."

Mrs. Guessner frowned. "Jamee, I know cheerleading is important to you. But the fact is even you won't be able to make the team if you fail this test."

Jamee nodded. It was probably too late already, she figured. With all the drama last night, she hadn't studied at all. What chance did she really have of passing the test? At least this way, she would know if she was good enough. And there was another reason she needed to be there today.

Angel.

"I know that, but I'm going to cheerleading tryouts. It's the last day," she said, thinking of all that happened already and all that still remained undone. "There's something important I have to do there."

"Do your parents know you're doing this?" Mrs. Guessner asked sternly.

Again, she knew she could lie, but she pushed it from her head. There had been enough of that already. "I don't think so."

"Jamee, I know you think I'm just trying to ruin your life, but honestly, I'm trying to help you. Your parents are, too. We're all very concerned. You're a bright girl, Jamee—as bright as your sister. But . . ." she sighed. "It's like you're trying to throw your future away."

Jamee shook her head. It wasn't the teacher's fault she didn't understand, but Jamee wasn't going to play games anymore.

"I'm not throwing my future away, Mrs. Guessner," Jamee said firmly. "It's just that I don't see my future like you do. Or like my parents do. Or like Darcy sees hers." She stood up straight and looked her teacher in the eyes. "I can't take the test this afternoon. I have to go to cheerleading tryouts. I'm sorry."

"I'm sorry, too, Jamee." Mrs. Guessner said with a heavy sigh. "Very sorry."

Chapter 8

"Have you seen Angel McAllister?" Jamee asked a group of girls standing in the locker room at the end of the day.

It had been one of the worst days at school she could remember. All day long, people were whispering and snickering about the picture. Sometimes they said things right to her face.

"Girl, could I get wit' that the next time you takin' pictures?" an older boy asked her in the lunch line, looking at her as if she were a car he wanted to drive. A few boys laughed along, as if they thought his comment was funny.

"You keep talkin' like that and you ain't never gonna get wit' anything," she said, acting strong, the way she did when she hung out with Bobby Wallace and his friends. And yet the truth was

that this boy's eyes made her nervous. She was glad when he left.

Later Jamee was scolded when she mistakenly bumped a girl in the cafeteria checkout line.

"You better step off. Just 'cause you like that doesn't mean I am, y'hear?" The girl almost seemed scared, and yet her eyes were angry, too.

Jamee was stunned. *What you think, I'm gonna bite you or something? Even if the rumors were true, it ain't right to hate on people!* she wanted to say.

She was sure Angel got the same treatment, and she hoped to speak to her at their table. But Angel never showed up at lunchtime. Jamee wondered if she had decided to skip school. Maybe the picture was too much and she quit cheerleading. The idea made Jamee even more furious with Vanessa. More than anyone, Angel deserved a chance to be on the squad. She had fought harder than anyone else over the last week. And somehow her success had become the one thing Jamee cared about in school, the one thing that pushed all her other problems out of her head.

"Have you seen Angel McAllister?" Jamee asked again. There were only a couple of girls in the locker room when she arrived. They looked nervous and barely acknowledged her.

"C'mon, people! Angel McAllister? She's about my height, wears glasses? Number thirty-five? The girl who did the aerial?"

"You mean the one in that *picture* with you?" one girl said knowingly. She was number twenty-two. Jamee couldn't remember her name.

"Yeah, her," Jamee said, bracing herself for another comment.

"You know, we was just talking about it, Nia and me." She nodded at the girl beside her. Jamee recognized her as a thicker-built girl who had surprisingly quick moves. "Isn't that our locker room in the background?"

Jamee nodded. It was the first time someone actually asked a question about the photo. Of course it would be another cheerleader, she thought. They knew the truth about what's been happening.

"All of us have had our tops off in here. Makes me want to change in the bathroom, just in case." She shook her head sympathetically.

"Me too, now," Jamee added.

"Who did this to you?" Nia spoke up then, looking around to make sure no one else was listening. "Was it that girl, Vanessa?"

Jamee nodded.

"Didn't I tell you, Marcie?" Nia said in a low voice. "That girl acts like she owns the cheerleaders, and Coach Seville ain't even picked any of us yet," she muttered, shaking her head. "Your name's Jamee, right?"

Jamee nodded again as Nia continued. "Well, we all been talking 'bout Vanessa. She's a piece of work. But like I told Marcie, she's the type who'll ruin your life if you stand up to her."

"Tell me about it," Jamee murmured. "But have you seen Angel?"

Nia shrugged toward the door. "I thought I saw somebody outside Coach Seville's office when I passed it—"

Jamee started moving. "Thanks!" she called to the two girls.

"Sure, Jamee. Good luck!"

Coach Seville's door was closed, but Angel was standing outside with her arms crossed on her chest and her head down when Jamee got there. She hadn't changed for practice or anything. Her face was blotchy and her eyes were red-rimmed. She looked as if she had been crying all day. She wanted to give her a hug—and even opened her arms—then decided against it because of the picture. Knowing that made Jamee feel angry all over again.

"Where were you today? I didn't see you at lunch."

"You think I wanted to be in that cafeteria on a day like this? Besides, you're better off without me. I'm sorry I dragged you into all this, Jamee," she sniffled.

"So what are you doing now?" Jamee asked her. "Please don't tell me you're quitting."

"Why not?" Angel sniffled. "That's what everyone wants, isn't it?"

"You can't quit. We're in the same boat, and I'm not gonna go out like that. We gotta find some way to make Vanessa and her friends admit this was all one big lie—"

"It doesn't matter if it's a lie!" Angel said angrily. "If everyone at this school believes it, it might as well be true. And we're not in the same boat, Jamee! *You* have friends. You have people who will stand up for you. People who know those rumors aren't true. You even have

132

a boyfriend!" Angel shook her head. "I don't have *anyone*."

"Well, I don't got a boyfriend anymore," Jamee told her. "We broke up this morning."

"Over the picture?"

Jamee hesitated. The picture played a part, but there was more there and Jamee knew it. "Not really," she said.

"Look, if you're trying to make me feel better, forget it. *Nothing* can make me feel better. I'm probably going to have to transfer *again!*" She brushed more tears off her face. "What's funny is, this summer, I promised myself that I was going to be different in high school, that I would try new things. When I heard about the auditions for cheerleading, I signed up before I could talk myself out of it. I should have known better," she said bitterly. "I should have known that girls like me don't get to be cheerleaders—"

"But Angel, look how far you've come!" Jamee pushed the picture from her mind and dropped an arm around Angel's shoulders. "None of this would've happened if you didn't have a real chance of making it. You're good. You just need to go out there and do it. And smile!"

Angel shook her head. "But everyone hates me! None of the girls will even speak to me—"

"*I'm* speaking to you! And so is Amberlynn. She knows it was a lie, just like she knows what they said about me isn't true. And I just talked to two other girls who don't believe it either! They just haven't said anything because they're scared—"

"Because if they say anything, they'll be next. And they're right, too. If you hadn't stuck up for me, this wouldn't be happening to you, either." Angel's voice shook with emotion. "Why do they hate me so much?"

Jamee rubbed Angel's shoulder the way Grandma used to do for her when she was upset. "Probably 'cause you remind them they ain't as special as they think they are," she answered. "That ain't a bad thing, Angel. Don't let the haters get you down." She meant the words to try to cheer Angel up, but saying them made her feel better, too.

Angel was silent. Jamee knew she was about to walk away and never come back.

"You can't quit, Angel. Let's finish this," she urged. "C'mon."

Just then Coach Seville's door swung open. The coach stepped out with her clipboard in hand but stopped when she saw them. "Something wrong?" she asked.

Jamee knew from her question that she hadn't seen the picture. Next to her, Angel took a deep breath and wiped her tears away. Her jaw suddenly looked firm, her eyes strong and clear.

"No, we're just a little nervous. That's all," Angel said.

Jamee smiled. She knew what it meant. Her talk worked. Angel wasn't quitting. She was going to audition.

Coach Seville eyed the girls briefly. "Let's save the tears until *after* I've posted the final results. For now, focus on the audition. Just do your best. Maybe there's no reason to cry. Okay?"

"Yes, Coach," Jamee and Angel answered together.

"Good. Now let's go!" she barked, clapping her hands as the two girls rushed to get dressed.

The hallway outside the gym buzzed with nervous chatter as Jamee and Angel approached. But as soon as they joined the line, it hushed. Jamee held her head up and tried to pretend she didn't care, but then Vanessa, Kym, and Renita sauntered over. Tasha was with them too, though her arms were crossed. She looked as if she would like to be somewhere else.

"Check it out. The lovers are here," Vanessa said, her voice just loud enough that everyone could hear it. Some snickered, but most were silent, as if they were gathering themselves for the audition.

"That's nasty," Renita said. Tasha remained silent, though Jamee thought she looked as if she wanted to say something.

Amberlynn joined the line and stood next to Angel, flashing Vanessa a dirty look.

"Uh oh. Looks like there's another one," Vanessa added.

"Yeah, maybe Angel's cheatin' on Jamee with her," said Kym.

"Imagine that," Vanessa said. "Jamee woulda lost a boyfriend *and* a girlfriend in one day!"

The girls cackled loudly. Jamee could feel herself sweating, her hands clenching into fists. She didn't know how long she could ignore Vanessa, and yet she knew if she talked back to her, it would end up in a fight. It would all be over.

Next to her, Angel seemed frozen. Not once did she glance back at Vanessa or her friends. Instead she focused on the gym, like a statue unable to turn her head, despite the laughter.

Hurry up, Jamee thought to herself, clenching her jaws. *Let's get this thing started!*

Finally, the gym door swung open, and Crystal the cheerleading captain appeared. Her eyes swept to Vanessa, Jamee, and Angel, but she didn't say anything. Jamee figured she had seen the picture.

"Get into your audition groups and wait to be called," she said. "Run in with spirit, do your jumps and any tumbling, then I'll count you off for the chant and routine. Finish up with more jumps. Coach Seville may ask you a few questions, then you're done. After your audition, you can leave. The results will be posted tomorrow on the bulletin board outside of the gym. Good luck!" She paused for a minute while the girls got into their groups. "Okay. Group one, let's go!"

A small group of four girls rose nervously. Jamee watched them bounce around a little before Crystal opened the gym door wide.

"Woo hoo!" the girls shouted as they all ran in, clapping and jumping. Then the door closed with a heavy thud. Someone had taped a piece of paper over the little window, so no one could see each other's audition, though Jamee could hear the cheers and the stomping of their step routine. She tried to imagine what she was going to do, but it was difficult because she kept hearing Vanessa and Kym's laughter in her head.

"Group two!" Crystal called.

"That's me," Amberlynn said. "But I'll be back. I'm not leaving until after you and Angel have your turns."

"Thanks, Amberlynn. Good luck." Jamee high-fived her.

"Yeah, good luck," Angel said.

"Why don't you give her a kiss, too," Kym said. "You know you want to."

"Yeah, especially since she won't be kissin' Dez no more," Vanessa added.

Jamee winced. She knew the girl was trying to mess her up just before her audition. *Don't let her win*, she told herself, trying to focus on her routine. But then another voice spoke up.

"How much did you pay for your hair,

Vanessa?" It was Angel.

Silence swept over the corridor where the girls were waiting. Vanessa's mouth dropped open as if she was stunned. She instinctively reached for her ponytail, as if trying to protect it.

"What?"

"Your hair," Angel repeated. "My mom's a stylist at Essentials Salon. That looks like one of the synthetics. Maybe $4.99 a track? Less if you can get it wholesale."

Gasps and hushed laughter erupted among the crowd of nervous girls.

Vanessa scowled, and her eyebrows seemed to meet in a straight line. She stepped closer to Angel with her hands clenched into fists.

"Hit her," Jamee said. "Hit her. Go 'head. Hit her and give me an excuse to beat you down. Hit her and there's no way you'll make cheerleader."

"You won't either," Vanessa said.

"Group three!" Crystal shouted.

Tasha stood up. As she headed for the gym door, she whispered, "Sit down, Vanessa. Don't you think you've done enough?" Then she pasted a big smile on her face and bounded into the gym, clapping and cheering as the heavy door slammed shut.

"Yeah, Vanessa. Sit down," Jamee said. "After all, your group is up next. You might need a minute to get your hair—I mean your head—together."

Vanessa cursed but stepped back and sat down. Jamee heard her whispering with Renita and Kym. Every few seconds she looked over with murder in her eyes, but Jamee didn't care. She would fail three more algebra tests just to see the look on her face when Angel stood up to her.

"Group four!"

Vanessa bounced up with her big fake smile on her made-up face and dashed into the gym. Before the heavy door swung closed, Jamee saw her do a perfect roundoff and jump up shouting "Go Bluford!" She was sure that Vanessa, as awful as she was, would make the team.

When Crystal shouted for group six, Jamee bounded into the gym, energized by what she had just witnessed—Angel standing up to Vanessa in front of everyone. The sight seemed to push her so she landed each flip, nailed each step, and hit each move as best she could, all with the biggest, most genuine smile she had in days. Coach Seville even said "Nice job" when she was done and didn't ask her any questions.

The only thing that didn't sit right was the way Crystal kept staring at her.

By the time she got back to the hallway, most of the girls were gone. Amberlynn was sitting with Angel, and Renita was by herself at the other end of the hall. Vanessa and Tasha were nowhere in sight.

"Group nine!" Crystal called at last, and Angel stood up.

"Thanks for waiting with me," she said.

"We'll be waiting when you come out to walk home together," Amberlynn said. "Give it all you've got!"

"Don't forget to smile," Jamee reminded her. There was no way to know how it went, except that before the gym door closed, Jamee could see Angel soar into the air in a perfect aerial.

"What if we all make it? You and me and Vanessa and Angel, too?" Amberlynn asked. "You know this isn't over."

Jamee sighed. She knew that even if she made the squad, she would probably be kicked off one way or another. But she wasn't ready to admit that yet.

"Let's just hope that doesn't happen," she answered, keeping her thoughts to herself.

"How was the test?" her mother asked as soon as she walked in the door. Jamee didn't know how to answer. Had Mrs. Guessner already called to say she hadn't taken it? Had Darcy told Mom what happened last night?

Jamee peered into her mother's face. She didn't look angry—or at least not as angry as she probably would be if she knew Jamee had gone to tryouts.

"Uh, fine I think," she answered.

"Good," Mom huffed. She was dressed for work and had her purse on her shoulder. "That's what I want to hear. Now you get to your room and get working on the rest of your schoolwork," she said. "Tomorrow night, I wanna sit down and talk with you about the things you said yesterday. But right now, I gotta go to work."

Jamee nodded as Mom rushed out the door. She knew another storm was coming.

Another call from Mrs. Guessner.

Another fight with her parents.

More proof she wasn't as good as

Darcy.

There was no stopping it now. But at least they had made it through auditions, she told herself, though Amberlynn's words haunted her. What if they all made the cut?

Chapter 9

Jamee found the bulletin board first thing Friday morning. Just as Coach Seville had promised, the winners were posted on a bright pink sheet of paper.

"Congratulations to you all," the note read. "The following girls should report for a brief meeting in the gym after school today."

Jamee's eyes darted to the names written in two neat columns on the sheet.

Amberlynn Bailey. Vanessa Pierce. Tasha Jenkins.

Of course they made it, Jamee thought as her eyes kept reading, her mouth dry and her heart pulsing. And then she saw them.

Angel McAllister, Jamee Wills. Renita and Kym were there, too. They had all made it, just as Amberlynn suggested.

Jamee sighed. After working so hard to be a cheerleader—and keeping Angel going—she wished she could be happy. But looking at the list told her that things would get no better. And if she got kicked off the team for her grades, they might even get worse, especially for Angel. Jamee knew she had to face Vanessa again and stop her. But how?

The bell snapped her from her thoughts, and Jamee dragged herself to algebra class, ignoring the snickers and stares that trailed behind her wherever she went.

Mrs. Guessner didn't say anything when she arrived. Instead, for the entire class, she acted as if Jamee didn't exist. It seemed as if the teacher had completely given up on her. In a way, it made Jamee feel worse than being nagged. Now, instead of being a bother to the teacher, she had become nothing. A lost hope. She could only imagine what Mom and Dad would say when they found out what she had done.

During English class, Jamee was startled when an office aide barged in.

"Jamee Wills, you need to go to Ms. Spencer's office right now," the aide said.

Jamee ignored the stares of her classmates and followed the aide to a stuffy conference room. Jamee could almost smell the countless meetings that happened there when students were expelled or suspended. Was she next?

Angel was already seated at the table, as were Coach Seville and Crystal. Ms. Spencer was at the head of the table.

"What's going on?" Jamee asked, alarmed at Angel's face. Her eyes were red and puffy, as if she had been crying. "What happened?"

"Something serious has been brought to my attention, Jamee," Ms. Spencer said sternly. "Very serious." She pulled out a cell phone, flipped it open and showed them the picture.

Jamee's face burned with embarrassment. She turned away from the image and the insulting caption underneath it.

"Crystal showed it to me at lunchtime, and I brought it straight to Ms. Spencer," Coach Seville explained, her voice tense and serious as if it were under great stress. "Girls, I'm not sure if you know how serious this is, but we have to get to the bottom of it right now."

"I'm sorry, Jamee," Crystal cut in. "But what happened wasn't right. I just kept thinking how I'd feel if someone did this to me, so I thought the right thing to do was to tell someone."

"It *was* the right thing to do, Crystal," said Ms. Spencer in a louder voice. "But you can return to your class now. The four of us will take care of this."

Crystal left and Ms. Spencer shut the heavy door behind her.

"Would you two like to tell us what's going on?" Ms Spencer asked. "Do you know who took and sent this picture?"

Jamee's palms were cold and clammy. Her stomach felt queasy. She felt trapped. Of course she was sure Vanessa and Tasha had done it, but she didn't want to tell on them. She wasn't like that. None of the people she grew up with were either, except maybe Darcy.

Jamee shrugged. She looked over at Angel and saw a tear stream from her eyes. Yet her mouth was shut too, probably because she feared what Vanessa, her friends, and the rest of Bluford High School would say about her if she snitched.

Coach Seville sighed, flipping her own cell phone in her hand. Jamee was sure she had the picture, too.

"I know this is hard for you girls," the coach said, "but Crystal has already given us the basic outline. We have to act, and if you don't help us, there will be a price to pay."

"Why us?" Jamee said. "We didn't do anything."

"Sending messages like this one over a cell phone is an act of bullying, and that will not be tolerated at this school," explained Ms. Spencer. "But taking a picture of teenage girls changing in a locker room and sending it to other teenagers—that's a crime. I'm about to call the police to get to the bottom of this, but I wanted to give you a chance to tell us what you know first."

Bullying. Police. Crime.

It made Jamee's head spin. It seemed as if each time she tried to get herself out of trouble, she only got in deeper. She could almost see Darcy staring at her and hear Aunt Charlotte's voice. *"I told you that girl wasn't gonna make it in high school, Mattie."*

"And if we find out the whole squad is involved in this, we're prepared to cancel cheerleading for the entire season," the principal added.

"Cancel cheerleading!" Jamee cried. She and Angel looked at each other.

"For everyone?" Angel asked.

"Absolutely," answered Ms. Spencer. "If the team hid the fact that others bullied and sent out inappropriate pictures, then yes, the entire squad can face discipline."

"Now do you understand how serious this is?" asked their coach. "Please be honest. I'm guessing you both know who's responsible, right?"

Angel cleared her throat. "They only did this because of me," she said. "If I never came here, none of this would have happened. I should just quit!"

"You ain't quitting, Angel," Jamee snapped. She thought over what Ms. Spencer and Coach Seville had said. She thought of Amberlynn and all of the other girls who worked so hard and had come so far. It didn't seem fair that none of them would get to represent Bluford on the cheerleading squad because of the actions of just a couple of people. There had to be a way to get it right, to make it so that Vanessa came forward and admitted what she did.

Suddenly, an idea flashed into her brain, a solution as complicated and calculated as any problem Mrs. Guessner wrote on her chalkboard.

"You're right, Coach Seville. Angel and I think we know who sent the message, but we don't want to accuse no one, either. But I think maybe we can make the person who did it come forward on her own. If you'll help us."

Ms. Spencer frowned. "How?"

Jamee explained. At first, she was afraid the principal would never go along with it. But in the end, Coach Seville whispered something in her ear and the two women nodded.

"Okay," Ms. Spencer said somberly. "We'll try it. But one way or another, we're gonna get to the bottom of this *today*. And if we have to cancel cheerleading to do it, we will."

"Listen up!" Coach Seville yelled to the girls crowded in the bleachers after school.

Crystal and some of the other cheerleaders closed the gym doors and stood watching, almost as if they were guarding something. Jamee could feel Vanessa and her friends huddled behind her like a wolf pack. She sat up a little straighter. Angel did, too. Everyone seemed tense, as if they knew something was about to happen.

"Usually, today I say 'congratulations' and we sit around and talk. Get to know each other better. But we're not going to do that today," she said abruptly. "Because there are some things going on in this group that need to stop." Coach Seville paused and pulled her cell phone out of her pocket and held it up.

Girls mumbled and shifted nervously in their seats. Jamee heard Tasha gasp.

"Things involving text messages and pictures and rumors about ladies who are members of this squad." She then explained what Ms. Spencer said, using the same words.

Bullying. Crime. Police.

"Our school policy required me to report this incident to Ms. Spencer this afternoon and to take action against the students responsible." She looked around the gym. "Would anyone like to be a real woman and tell me what she knows?"

Just as Jamee expected, the crowd was silent. All the whispers and the rude comments she had heard for a week were gone. The only sound was the occasional creak of the bleachers as someone shifted in her seat.

"I see," Coach Seville continued icily, snapping her phone closed and pacing in front of the bleachers. She stopped near Jamee and glared at the crowd of girls for a moment. Jamee could almost feel her face burn from the intensity of the coach's stare.

"I've gotta be honest with you girls," the coach confessed. "If I hadn't seen the messages myself, I'da told Ms. Spencer, 'Sorry, but no one on my squad did that. Not my girls.' But I guess I don't know some of you the way I thought I did."

The coach's words seemed to hang in the air. Jamee glanced at Angel. She sat motionless, her eyes focused on an invisible spot on ground.

"I still can't believe someone on this squad would violate her teammate by taking a picture of her while she's undressed," boomed the coach. "And I'm furious that she then sent the picture around school and made jokes about her teammate's sexuality. I don't care who you are or where you come from, you have no right to go there," Coach Seville thundered, filling the gym with her voice.

"But you know what angers me the most? That some of you knew what was happening and did nothing about it.

What would you do if it was *you* being targeted? Would you want people to look the other way? No you wouldn't. You'd pray someone stood up for you."

The girls on the bleachers were like statues as Coach Seville paced.

"We're a team, ladies. We don't hate on each other. We don't tear each other down. And if we see someone doing that, we don't walk away. You hear me? If you can't handle that, you don't belong here."

Coach Seville paused. Jamee knew what was coming next, and yet she still felt nervous.

"Now, unless we get to the bottom of this, none of you will be allowed to cheer for Bluford. We're suspending the program for a year."

"*What?*"

"Are you *serious?!*"

"That ain't right!"

Just as Jamee figured, the bleachers erupted with protests. She glanced at Vanessa. Her mouth was open in surprise. A few other girls started whispering, all the while casting looks in Vanessa's direction.

"B-but Coach Seville!" Tasha's voice rose over the rest. "What if we didn't have nothing to do with it? It's not fair to punish all of us because of what some-one else did."

"Then what you all need to do is find out who did it and let me know. You have one hour."

"An *hour?!*" someone yelled. Others mumbled and whispered angrily.

"That's long enough for you to figure it out. Help each other. That's what a good team does. If one member is attacked, you're all attacked. How can we build a pyramid on the field if you don't trust each other? How can you fall from the top of the pyramid if you can't trust who will catch you? Now someone is spreading some hurtful stuff about two of your teammates. It's wrong and cowardly and has no place on this squad. If you work together to find out who's doing this, you'll grow as a team and be successful. If not, you'll have a year to think about it."

The crowd grumbled again, and Coach Seville gazed at them with a grim, knowing smile.

"Good luck, girls. I'll be back with Ms. Spencer in an hour," she said and walked out.

Chapter 10

Everyone looked at each other in silence.

Amberlynn, Angel, and Jamee stared hard at Vanessa. And for the first time, so did Kym, Renita, and Tasha. Jamee noticed that several of the other girls were watching her too, including Nia and Marcie, the two girls she had spoken to yesterday.

"Well," Vanessa said when the room got heavy with tension. "I guess you've ruined it for all of us, Tasha."

"What?" Tasha cried. "*Me?*"

Vanessa shrugged. "You're the one who's always bragging about your phone. Weren't you taking pictures with it in here the other day?"

"I can't believe you!" Tasha howled. "I might have taken the picture, but I didn't do nothing with it! The whole thing was *your* idea, Vanessa. You're the one who wants to control the whole cheerleading squad. You're the one who hated Angel from the start. You sent the—"

"Great," Vanessa rolled her eyes. "Now that you're about to get caught, you're going to blame *me*?" She shook her head. "I don't even have a cell phone. This is all you, girl, and you know it. Ain't that right?"

Renita and Kym nodded, but neither of them looked up at anyone in the group.

Tasha's face crumpled. "I know it looks bad, Angel, but I'm telling you, I didn't do it!" she wailed. "I know I was kind of mean to you before, and I did take that picture. But I never sent it around the school. I swear."

"I believe you," Angel said.

Tasha looked relieved. "Thank you, Angel," she said. "I'm serious. I'm not lying—"

"Yes you are," Vanessa interrupted. "All Coach Seville has to do is look at the messages you sent and she'll see—"

"You seem to know an awful lot about her phone, Vanessa."

Jamee had been thinking the same thing, but it was Nia who said it. She

156

folded her arms over her chest and shook her head. "We've all seen you borrow it from her a bunch of times."

"And maybe the reason you know what the teachers are gonna find is 'cause you put it there," added Nia's friend Marcie.

Vanessa rolled her eyes. "Girl, I know because she *told* me what she was gonna do." Once again, she looked back at Kym and Renita. "You guys were there. Remember when she told us?"

"Why do you keep asking them?" Another girl spoke up this time. "It's like you can't even say a sentence unless you have someone to back you up."

"I don't need *anyone* to back me up." Anger tainted Vanessa's voice. "I'm just telling you all what happened so we can stay on the team—"

"No, you're just tellin' us your version so *you* can stay on the team," Amberlynn said. "I've seen how you been treating Angel. Even if Tasha did it, you were running the show. I wouldn't trust either of you behind my back when I'm getting changed. How am I gonna know you ain't takin' pictures of me?" A number of girls mumbled in agreement.

"Didn't you listen?" Vanessa snapped.

"Tasha just said she took the picture!"

"But she said *you're* the one who sent it," Angel cut in.

"And I told you I didn't!" Vanessa hissed, her eyes pointed like two daggers aimed at Angel. "Kym and Renita got my back, so whatcha gonna say now?"

"They're lying! They're all lying," Tasha protested. "I didn't do it."

"Yeah, whatever," Vanessa scoffed, studying the crowd of girls staring at her. "I don't believe Coach Seville anyway. They can't cancel cheerleading. They're just trying to scare us. Even though you did it, Tasha, I ain't gonna say anything. If you all knew what was good for you, you wouldn't say nothing neither." Vanessa crossed her arms and acted as if she was above everyone else, in charge somehow.

Jamee could see Vanessa calculating, trying to find a way to save herself. She knew Vanessa would never come out and tell the truth. Jamee had counted on it.

"What if you're wrong?" Kym said then.

"Yeah, it wouldn't be the first time," added Renita.

"Then we tell her the truth," Vanessa

said with a sly smile. "Tasha did it."

Thunk!

The steel gym door clicked and swung open. Coach Seville marched in with Ms. Spencer right behind her. Jamee saw a cell phone in the principal's hand.

"Well, ladies," Coach's voice sounded even louder in the stillness that fell over the group. "Ms. Spencer is aware of our problem." She paused. "Have you determined who is responsible?"

There was a long silence. Jamee wanted to say something, but she knew she couldn't. One of the other girls would have to speak up. Tasha shifted nervously, and Jamee could see that she wanted to tell the truth, but Vanessa's threat seemed to work. Tasha didn't say a word. Angel shifted nervously next to her.

Jamee glanced over at Marcie and Nia, then at Kym and Renita, and the rest of the new cheerleaders. All their heads were down. Their eyes seemed to be glued to the floor. The only other person with her head up was Vanessa. She stared around the room like the silence meant she had won something. Jamee couldn't take it. She had to act now.

"Coach Seville?" she asked, standing up in her seat. "I know that you're trying to help us, and I understand you're trying to teach us about teamwork. But these girls have worked hard to be on this squad. I don't think it would be fair for all of them to lose their places just because someone don't like me. So I quit." She stepped off the bleachers and stood alone on the floor.

Murmurs spread across the bleachers.

"Jamee?" Coach Seville shook her head. "I can't stop you, if that's your choice. But that doesn't solve our problem—"

"I'm quitting, too," Angel stood up and joined her. "Jamee's right. It's not fair."

"I can't be on the team if these girls leave," Amberlynn spoke up. "They didn't do anything wrong. Besides, I don't want to cheer with people I don't trust."

"Me either," Nia said.

"Or me," added Marcie.

Two more girls popped up after them and then several more. They came to stand with Jamee and Angel. Soon Vanessa, Kym, Renita, and Tasha were the only ones left sitting on the bleachers.

Tasha stood up then. "I really wanted

to be a Bluford cheerleader, and I worked hard for it, but I did something wrong and stupid. I . . . took the pictures—"

Murmurs erupted from the crowd. Tasha raised her voice to speak over them.

"But I never sent them, Coach Seville. I swear. I lent my phone to Vanessa and she—"

"You're lying, Tasha!" Vanessa screeched. "Tell them she's lying. Kym? Renita?"

All eyes in the gym focused on them. Under the scrutiny, they seemed to shrink. For a moment, the gym was silent. Finally Kym broke the silence.

"It's gone too far, Vanessa. It ain't right to blame Tasha alone for what *you* did." She then turned to Coach Seville. "We were there, Renita and me. We saw Vanessa send the pictures from Tasha's phone."

"No! They didn't," Vanessa fumed. "They're just blaming me to save themselves!"

"Vanessa, just let it go. It's over," Renita said.

"Tasha, I'm going to need to see your phone," Ms. Spencer said gravely. "Come with me to my office, Vanessa.

Kym and Renita, you're coming, too. We need to have a long talk."

The girls filed out of the gym with their heads down. Vanessa shot Jamee an angry look, but it didn't matter. The truth was finally out. Vanessa had been caught. The fight was over. The gym door slammed shut and the four girls were gone.

"Congratulations, ladies," Coach Seville shouted. "You've just become a team."

The coach then began to clap. Crystal and the other senior cheerleaders joined in. Then the applause spread to the girls on the gym floor who had left the bleachers, girls who were ready to quit the team because they felt it was the right thing to do.

Jamee felt a lump in her throat as the applause grew louder and seemed to focus on her until the gym itself echoed with the roar of hands clapping.

"Excellent!" the coach said. "I'll see you all Monday right after school for our first practice. Congratulations again!"

The cheerleaders began dispersing and heading back into the hallway. Jamee was about to join them when she heard the coach call out to her.

"Jamee, can I see you for a minute?"

She had expected the coach to smile and to say something about how they had handled Vanessa, but Coach Seville's expression was grim.

"Jamee, Mrs. Guessner spoke with me and Principal Spencer a little while ago." She winced as if what she had to say pained her. "I'm afraid we have another problem."

"I can't believe it!" Jamee's father yelled. "After everything your mother and I talked about, you *still* disobeyed us!"

Jamee didn't even try to defend herself, not when her parents were this upset.

"Mrs. Guessner called me at work, Jamee," her mother chimed in. "At *work!* I thought something bad had happened. Scared me half to death! Then to find out you been lying to us again?"

"Calm down, Mattie. You know it ain't good for you to get so upset."

"How can I *not* be upset, Carl?" Jamee's mother cried. "I don't know what's wrong with this child. We tell her to do something, and she goes off and does whatever she wants to." She shook her head. "You and your sister couldn't be more different." She pointed at Darcy. "Darcy's been working hard all afternoon on her schoolwork, while you were out there jumping around with your friends!"

"Mom, Dad," Darcy interrupted. "That's not fair. There's a lot going on at school right now—"

"I don't care *what's* going on at school, Darcy," her mother snapped. "That's no excuse to lie to us, to lie to a teacher, and to accept an *F* when a teacher offered to help her. What's the matter with you, Jamee? Don't you care about your future? You wanna fail ninth grade? Is that what you want?"

Jamee slumped in the living room chair. Did they even want her answer? She had tried to explain once, but her parents were just too angry to listen. Angry because they left their jobs, angry because they couldn't afford to miss work with a baby on the way, angry because they had been lied to. Jamee heard it all already.

"Well, is that it?" her mother demanded. "You've got nothing to say?"

"There's more to life than school and grades, Mom, okay? I wish you guys could just see that and be proud of me for what I'm good at—"

"What? Doin' splits?" her mother said. "That ain't gonna get you into college."

The comment stung. Jamee felt as if Mom had kicked her in the stomach. She couldn't speak.

"But Mom. I spoke to her friend Crystal," Darcy interrupted again. "There really *is* something you should know—"

"Stop trying to defend her, Darcy!" Mom cried. "We told her to take that test after school yesterday and she didn't do it! What else is there to say?" She leveled a finger at Jamee's face. "From now on, home and school. That's it, Jamee. No cheerleading, no football games, no Niko's, no boys, no *nothing*. Understand?"

No cheerleading.

Jamee had suspected it from the beginning, but the words still hurt. They were taking away the one thing she enjoyed, the one thing she liked about school, the one place where she had fought for something important and won. Her parents would never understand that.

She nodded slowly, holding back the tears that gathered in her eyes. "Can I go to my room now?"

Her father sighed as if someone had

settled a heavy weight on his back, as if Jamee was suddenly a burden to him. "Go. We'll talk more about this later." Mom complained some more, something about not having guests over, but Jamee didn't listen. She headed down the hall toward her room, barely hearing the doorbell ring.

Jamee passed Grandma's room, gazing at the awful emptiness where her grandmother used to live. *If only she were still alive*, Jamee thought. *She'd listen. She'd understand.*

Voices filled the living room as Jamee reached her doorway. She thought she recognized one. Could it be? She turned around and headed back.

A woman stood in her living room. Next to her was Angel and her little sister, Dionne. Both girls smiled as Jamee approached.

"You must be Jamee," said the woman. Her face was just like Angel's—round and smooth but without glasses. The rest of her was round and soft too, as if she had a pillow tied to her stomach beneath her purple dress. The woman moved quickly toward Jamee and took her hand. "When Angel told me about what you did today, I just had to come and thank you. Monday morning, I'm gonna go over to that school and tell the principal and the coach and anybody else that needs tellin' that this girl shouldn't be punished for what she did. They ought to give her a medal!"

"I hope you're not mad," Angel added quietly. "But Amberlynn told me about Mrs. Guessner and the algebra test. I told my mom everything. Maybe after Mrs. Guessner finds out what happened, they'll let you back on the team."

Jamee shook her head. "It won't matter. My parents are making me quit."

"*Quit?*" Angel said. "Why?"

"After all she done, she's gonna *quit*? That don't make any sense," said Angel's mother.

Jamee felt her parents staring at her.

"Done?" Dad asked, his brow crinkled in confusion. "What did she do?"

"She got those mean bully girls to leave my sister alone!" Dionne exclaimed in a loud childish voice.

"It's true," Angel said, then launched into the full story from the beginning. From time to time, Jamee's parents interrupted to ask questions, but mostly they listened. Every now and then, one of them would glance at Jamee as if they had never seen her before.

"That girl Vanessa is *scary*," Darcy added. "If I were a freshman, you wouldn't catch me near her. I don't know how you stood up to her all this time. I'd a stayed out of her way."

"That's 'cause you're smarter than me," Jamee answered.

"So that's why you skipped the test?" Jamee's father asked. "So you could confront these girls after school?"

"I just didn't want Angel to quit because of them," Jamee said, squirming under all the attention. "And I couldn't let them think that I'd quit because of them. It didn't seem right."

"But why didn't you tell that to your teacher? Or us?"

"Mrs. Guessner wouldn't understand."

"But *we* would have," Mom said. "Why didn't you tell us?"

"I tried," Jamee shrugged. "But you wouldn't listen. I was wasting my time 'doing splits,' remember? All you, my teachers, and Aunt Charlotte want is another Darcy. I told you. I can't be her, Mom. I'm someone else." As she spoke, Jamee felt her eyes stinging, but she blinked back her tears.

Her parents looked at each other.

Dad shook his head heavily. Mom's eyes widened as if she figured out something that had been a mystery to her. The frustration on their faces moments ago suddenly disappeared. In its place was something else. Concern. Appreciation. Understanding. Instantly Mom reached out and hugged her.

"You got it all wrong, Jamee," Mom blurted. "But it's our fault. We love you so much. We just wanna see you make it in this world, to be happy, that's all. That's why we push so hard. But we got so caught up in everything goin' on around here, we stopped listening to you. And for that we're sorry. You hear me?"

Mom's hands held Jamee's face. She could feel the warmth of Mom's palms sinking into her, the pressure of Mom's pregnant belly pressing gently into her stomach.

Jamee nodded, her throat suddenly tight, her eyes moist.

"I know what it's like to be in your sister's shadow. I felt like that my entire childhood," Mom admitted. "I never wanted to put that burden on you."

Dad was there, too. Jamee felt his hand rub her back. "It's tough out here in the adult world. Believe me, I know. Getting your education is one way to make sure you don't end up like me, struggling for work all the time, worrying about bills," he explained. "But there are more important things in this world than grades. You just reminded us of that today, and we're proud of you."

"Me too. Like I said, I could never do what you did today," Darcy said sincerely, hugging her.

Jamee was speechless. In the embrace, Jamee felt the resentment and anger she'd carried for so long beginning to thaw. For a moment, the living room was quiet.

"Well," Mrs. McAllister said, stepping toward the door. Jamee had almost forgotten that she and her family were still there. "We got to be going. We just had to come by and say thanks. And Jamee, on Monday, I'm gonna talk to your teacher. She needs to know what's been going on."

"We'll be there, too, Mrs. McAllister," said Mom. "Maybe we can turn this thing around."

Angel gave Jamee a quick hug. "See you Monday at lunch?"

"I'll be there," Jamee said, hugging

her back hard. "Thanks, Angel."

When the door closed, Mom wrapped her arms around Jamee again. "We got a lot to talk about. But I promise you from now on, we'll be listening. But you gotta promise me something back. You're gonna do your best. You don't need to be Darcy. But you do need to be the best that *Jamee* can be."

Jamee closed her eyes. For the first time in weeks, she felt her family was on her side. The lies were gone. Finally everyone knew what she had faced, what she had accomplished, and what mattered to her.

"If I do, can I cheer?" she asked.

Jamee saw the answer in their eyes and felt the soaring aerials in her heart.

Have you read these new Bluford Series books?

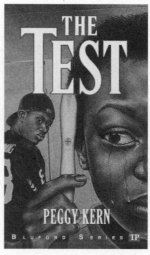

For more information, visit
www.townsendpress.com